THE GUNSMITH

442

The Last Wagon Train

Books by J.R. Roberts
(Robert J. Randisi)

The Gunsmith series

Lady Gunsmith series

Angel Eyes series

Tracker series

Mountain Jack Pike series

COMING SOON!

The Gunsmith
443 – Beauty and the Gun

For more information visit:
www.SpeakingVolumes.us

THE GUNSMITH

442

The Last Wagon Train

J.R. Roberts

SPEAKING VOLUMES, LLC
NAPLES, FLORIDA
2018

The Last Wagon Train

ISBN 978-1-62815-952-3

Chapter One

Denver, CO

Under normal circumstance a visit to Denver always meant Clint Adams would spend time with his friend, Talbot Roper. This time was no different. Clint had been on the trail for a while. Some of that time was a favor to Roper, who had needed help with a job. Now he was ready to stop in a city, sleep in a comfortable bed, eat at restaurants, and even go to the theater. And maybe even buy a new suit.

When Clint checked in at his usual hotel, The Denver House, there was already a message from Roper.

"Nice to see you again, Mr. Adams," the clerk said. "I have a message for you."

"Thank you," Clint said, accepting it. "Can I get my usual room?"

"Of course," the clerk said. "Those are my instructions, you know. Whenever you check in, you get the same room."

"Thanks," Clint said, accepting the key.

"And, as usual, you don't need help carrying your luggage to your room?"

"No," Clint said, indicating his one carpetbag, "I don't."

"Have a nice stay, sir."

"Thanks."

The Denver House was the only hotel in the United States where Clint Adams secured a room that actually overlooked the main street. He didn't expect to be shot from a rooftop or window across the street, but he also didn't intend to spend a lot of time in front of the window. He simply enjoyed having an occasional look at the street from two stories up.

He unpacked his bag, putting his several articles of clothing into the dresser drawers and hanging one jacket in the closet. He was going to have to ask Roper for the name of a good clothing store.

That thought reminded him of the message the clerk had given him. He unfolded it and found it was from Roper.

"Sorry, emergency case called me out of town. See you next time."

"Damn," Clint said, setting the message aside. "Steak dinner alone."

Clint decided to stay in Denver for at least a week anyway, so he started eating in different places—new places he had never tried before, except for breakfast in the Denver House diningroom. He also found a store where he bought two new suits, which he wore to several theaters and dance halls.

One of the halls he went to was the Immigrant Saloon and Dance Hall, which was advertising a performance by the famous singer Sally Songbird. It couldn't have been a real name, but he was willing to go and listen to her sing. So he donned one of his new suits and headed out for an evening of steak, beer and music.

***

As he arrived outside the Immigrant, he saw there was a line of people entering. The only way to get in was to join the line. Of course, that was if he wanted to hear the songbird sing. But there was another door which led into the saloon and gambling hall part of the building. He decided to go in that way rather than wait in a line.

The saloon was busy, with all the seats at the gaming tables taken, and not much space to be had at the bar. Of course, that's what elbows were for.

Clint went to the bar, elbowed himself some room and got the bartender's attention. He wasn't wearing his holster, but he had his Colt New Line, the little .22 he used, stuck into his belt at the small of his back. Hopefully, there wouldn't be any reason for him to use it.

He picked up his beer mug, turned and watched the activity across the floor. The men who weren't gambling were watching, or sitting at tables, drinking together. The pretty saloon girls were working the floor, wearing brightly colored dresses and carrying trays of drinks to smiling customers. It looked as if they had all been hired for their looks. Most saloons made sure they hired girls of all sizes, shapes and hair color. The Immigrant was no different. There was a tall, slender brunette, a chubby, busty blonde, and a short redhead, all wearing smiles on their beautiful faces.

"Look at this fella here," someone said. "Ain't he dressed fancy."

Clint tuned his head, saw that the speaker was a man in his 30s, who was apparently talking about him to his friends at the bar. They were all dressed as if they had come directly from their jobs—clean clothes, but nothing fancy. Certainly nothing like the suit Clint was wearing, which the man seemed to be referring to.

"You talking to me, friend?" Clint asked.

"Not talkin' to you, actually," the man said, "but talkin' about you and your fancy clothes. Where d'ya think you are?"

"I know where I am," Clint said. "I'm in Denver. I'm going next door to hear a songbird sing in a theater where a suit like this is fitting."

"But you're here, havin' a beer in the saloon?" the man said. "That suit's outta place here."

"That's not for you to decide, friend," Clint said.

"Who the hell are you?" the man asked. "See, we belong here. We come here a lot. Far as I know, you ain't never been here before, and you don't belong here now. In fact, you're drinkin' a beer that belongs to somebody else."

Clint looked at the beer in his hand, then back at the man.

"So you want me to put this beer down?"

The man looked at his smiling friends, 4 of them, which made it a gang of 5 Clint was facing.

"Drake," the bartender said to the man, "not in here, fella."

"You shut up, Wendell," Drake said, "this ain't got nothin' to do with you."

Clint looked at the bartender, Wendell, who shrugged helplessly as if to say, "Hey, I tried."

Clint looked back at Drake and his friends. He didn't see any guns, but he did see 3 knives, one of which was on Drake's belt. The other 4 men were Drake's age, and Clint had the feeling that all of them worked together.

"Look, fellas," Clint said, "I didn't come here looking for trouble. How about I buy all of you a beer—"

"How about you put that one down, turn around and walk out," Drake said. "That's what we want."

Clint was puzzled. These men weren't even drunk, and they didn't seem to know who he was. Those would have been the only 2 reasons he could think of for this or was this just something they pulled each night on an unsuspecting customer?

"So you don't want me to drink this beer," Clint said.

"No," Drake said, "we want you to put it down. Put it on the bar and walk out."

Clint looked at the beer in his hand, then took 2 steps forward, poured the beer out onto Drake's boots, and set the empty mug down on the bar, then stepped back.

"There you go," Clint said. "I didn't drink it."

"You just made a big mistake, Mister," Drake said, his face growing red.

"I think you're going to find out that the mistake was yours," Clint told him.

Chapter Two

The 5 men moved away from the bar, spreading out. The people around them withdrew, giving as much space as they could.

"Is five-to-one your idea of fair odds?" Clint asked.

"Hey," Drake said, "we gave you a chance to put the beer down and walk away."

"And now I'm giving you a chance to do the same," Clint said. "Walk away."

"Too late," Drake said, and drew the knife from his belt.

On either side of him the men also drew their knives, all of which were large and sharp, and reflected the lights around them.

The other 2 men were big and muscular, so they simply flexed the fingers of their large hands, then closed them into fists.

"Looks like you fellows like to fight," Clint said. "I don't like to fight."

"So," Drake said, "you're a coward, huh?"

"No," Clint said, reaching behind him and coming out with the New Line. "I like guns."

The 5 men stopped and stared at the gun.

"You won't shoot us," Drake said, nervously.

"Why not?" Clint asked. "You think I'm going to take a beating from five idiots?"

Drake eyed the gun, which was steady in Clint's hand, and said, "That ain't fair."

"You're standing there with four friends, and knives, talking about what's fair?"

The 5 men were exchanging glances, obviously wondering what to do next.

"Now be good boys and get out of here," Clint said. To emphasize his words, he cocked the hammer on the gun.

"You think we're afraid of that little gun?" Drake said.

"I know you better be," Clint said. "There are five of you, and I've got a bullet for each of you in here."

"Whataya think this is, the Wild West?" Drake demanded.

"Don't be an idiot for the rest of your life, Drake," Wendell the bartender said, "which ain't gonna be too long. That's Clint Adams."

"What?" Drake said, instantly recognizing the name.

"The Gunsmith," Wendell said.

Leave it to a bartender to recognize him, Clint thought.

Drake looked at him.

"Are you . . . him?"

"It doesn't matter who I am," Clint said. "I'm holding a gun."

Drake allowed the knife to fall from his hand.

"Hey, listen," he said, "we didn't mean nothin'—"

"Pick up your knife and get out," Clint said.

"Yeah, yeah, s-sure," Drake said. He picked the knife up, stuck it back in its sheath, and led the way to the door. The other 4 followed him, quickly.

Clint stuck the gun back into his belt. Customers started coming back to the bar, but they gave him room.

"Another beer?" Wendell asked. "On the house?"

"You bet."

Wendell drew it and set it down in front of Clint.

"I hope you don't mind," the bartender said, "but I didn't want blood on the floor tonight."

"Well, it worked," Clint said, "so I guess I don't mind." He saw customers looking, and saloon girls staring at him. "Although I did sort of like the anonymity I thought I had."

"Sorry about that."

Clint took a deep gulp of cold beer. The smell of perfume touched his nostrils before he even noticed the girl approaching him. It was the chubby blonde, who was staring at him with wide, blue eyes.

"Mister," she said, "that was so brave."

"You think so?" he asked her. "I had a gun and they didn't. How brave was that?"

"Would you have shot them?" she asked.

"If I had to," he admitted. "Luckily, I didn't. What's your name?"

"I'm Melanie."

"Well Melanie, tell me, what are the chances of getting in next door without waiting in line?" he asked.

She grinned and pointed at Wendell.

"You're askin' the wrong person," she said. "But Wendell can get you in, and at a seat up front."

"How much?" Clint asked.

"Don't worry about it," Wendell said. "I'll take care of it."

"Why? Do you own the place?"

"Oh no," Wendell said, "but I got the right to take anybody I want into the theater, no charge." He came around the bar and stood next to Clint. "Just follow me."

Wendell started off. Clint drank half the beer, set the mug down, said thank you to pretty Melanie, and hurried after him.

Chapter Three

Sally Songbird lived up to her name.

Wendell walked Clint right to the front row, center seat, and then told him to come back and have a drink when the show was over.

People seated behind him gave him strange looks, as did the people on either side, but he didn't pay any attention to them. Especially when Sally Songbird finally came out. She was an ash blonde and beautiful, but when she opened her mouth and began to sing, he forgot about that. From that point on, she was just a voice.

After she was finished, she walked off the stage to thunderous applause, and people started to leave. Clint waited until most of them were gone or, at least, at the back of the theater, then he went to the side and used the same special door Wendell had used to bring him in.

"How was it?" Wendell asked, when he got back to the bar.

"Fascinating, actually," Clint said. "The lady can really sing."

"I know," Wendell said. "I heard her before."

"Was it you who recommended her for this performance?" Clint asked.

"Naw," Wendell said. "The boss doesn't put any stock in what I think. He makes his own decisions."

"Who is the boss?" Clint asked.

"His name is Calvin Morehead," Wendell said. "He owns a couple of places, but this is the biggest one."

"Good for him," Clint said. He finished his beer and set the mug down. "Thanks for the beer, Wendell, and the great seat. She's amazing."

"Yeah, she is."

"I'll say good-night now," Clint said.

"Really?" Wendell asked. "There's a poker game I know of—"

"I'm trying to take some time off from the things I usually do," Clint said. "Poker's one of them. But thanks, anyway."

"Well," Wendell said, "come on back anytime."

"I will."

Clint left the Immigrant and went back to his hotel.

***

He'd been in Denver almost a week and, still without Talbot Roper, he was running out of things to do—restaurants to eat in, saloons to go to, theaters. And nothing he had seen had matched the performance of Sally Songbird.

So on the morning of the 8th day, he was considering checking out of the hotel and heading for the railroad station. He had left Eclipse in the care of Rick Hartman in Labyrinth, Tx., and was starting to miss the big Darley Arabian.

He had almost made his decision to pack his bag when there was a knock on the door. In fact, the empty bag was open and sitting on the bed. Grabbing his Peacemaker from his holster, he carried it to the door.

"Who is it?"

"Melanie, from the Immigrant."

Clint opened the door, peered out, saw the chubby girl standing there, alone. He opened the door the rest of the way and peered out. The first time he had seen her she was wearing a blue dress that showed a lot of her creamy shoulders. This time she was wearing red, and it not only showed shoulder, but the upper slopes of her large breasts.

"I'm alone," she said.

"Just checking," Clint said. "Come on in."

Melanie entered, looked down at the gun Clint was holding.

"Sorry," Clint said, "it's a force of habit. I don't answer any doors without my gun."

"Guess I can't blame you for that."

Clint figured that the girl was not armed, so he walked to the bed and holstered the gun.

"What can I do for you, Melanie?"

"I have a message for you."

"From who?"

"Mr. Morehead."

Clint stared at her.

"My boss?"

"I know who he is," Clint said. "What's the message?"

"He'd like you to come and see him."

"What for?"

"He wants to hire you."

"To do what? I don't hire my gun out."

"Nothin' like that," Melanie said. "He'll tell ya when he sees ya."

"Why doesn't he come to me?"

"He doesn't want people to know he's seein' ya," Melanie said.

"Then how do I get to see him?"

"He suggests you come to the Immigrant tonight for a drink," Melanie said. "Then I'll take you to his office."

"Do you have any idea what he wants?" Clint asked. "I was thinking of leaving Denver today."

"He's willin' to pay you for your time," Melanie said, "even if you don't take the job."

"I'm not looking for a job," Clint said. "The money's not important."

"Okay, then," Melanie said. "maybe he just wants to ask you for a favor. You do favors for people, don't ya?"

"I've been known to, on occasion," Clint admitted.

"Then come by the Immigrant tonight," Melanie said. "You'll get a beer on the house, and it'll be worth your while."

Clint hesitated.

"I bet it'll be interestin'," she added.

"Well," Clint said, "I could use something interesting."

"So, how's 8 p.m.?" Melanie asked.

"You tell your boss, Mr. Morehead," Clint replied, "that I'll be at the Immigrant at 8 p.m."

"That's great!" Melanie said.

But the saloon girl didn't make a move toward the door.

"Was there something else, Melanie?"

"Well," she said, pressing her hands together in front of her, "I was just thinkin' we could make things interestin' right now."

"And how would we do that?" he asked.

"Well," she said, letting her hands glide around behind her, "we could start by me takin' off this dress."

15

Chapter Four

The dress came off very quickly, and he stared at the acres of pale flesh that had been beneath it. The girl was chubby all over—heavy upper arms, big, pink-tipped breasts, lovely, solid thighs and calves, and she turned to show him the twin cheeks of her big, round butt.

There was absolutely nothing wrong with her. The girl was built for bed.

She approached Clint, then, and began to undo his belt and trousers, sliding them to his ankles along with his underwear. Since his boots were already off, he was able to step right out of his pants. She went to her knees and took his already hard cock into her right hand, stroking it, while fondling his sack with her left.

"Mmmm," she said, "this is gonna be interestin'."

"You're right about that," he said. "You're a beautiful girl, Melanie."

"And you got a beautiful tallywacker, Mr. Gunsmith," she said.

She leaned forward, opened her mouth, took the head of his cock inside, wetting it, then letting it pop out, while still stroking him with her hand. She licked it, then ran her tongue along one side of his length, and up the other side, getting him shiny with her saliva, then taking him in again, only deeper, this time.

She moved her hands to his thighs, ran them up the back until she reached his butt. She grabbed both cheeks and pulled him to her, so she could get his cock as deeply into her mouth as she could. From there she began bobbing her head back and forth, letting her lips glide over him. He reached down to touch her head, her hair so blonde it was almost white. He noticed that her shoulders and the back of one arm were dotted with brown beauty marks.

Finally, she released him from her mouth, gave the head of his penis a last lick, then stood up and kissed him. She was tall, probably about 5'9", and she filled his arms with smooth, hot flesh. Her mouth was avid, her tongue active, and they kissed for a long time, with her occasionally moaning into his mouth. Between them, his hard penis pulsed against her soft belly.

Still locked in a hot kiss they moved to the bed together. Before they fell onto it, she broke the kiss and stepped back.

"You don't mind that I'm fat, right?"

He looked down at his rigid cock and said, "Does this look like I mind? Besides, you're not fat. You're beautiful."

She stared at him, then smiled and rushed him, they fell onto the bed. He managed to flip her over onto her back, began to kiss her neck, shoulders, and breasts. He took those pink nipples into his mouth and didn't want to let them go. He sucked, flicked them with his tongue, while she moaned and writhed beneath him.

He continued, then, to run his mouth and tongue over her smooth skin, down over the large expanse of her belly, down between her thighs.

He peppered her soft inner thighs with kisses before centering his attention on her wet vagina. He licked the length of it, tasting her, causing her to gasp and stiffen. She reached down to grasp his head as he continued to use his tongue, lips and finger on her, bringing her to a shuddering climax that left her breathless and teary eyed.

"Omigod!" she gasped.

"Isn't that what you came here for?" he asked, looking up from between her thighs.

"No," she said, "I came to give you pleasure."

He laid beside her on the mattress.

"Well, you can still do that," he said. "We're in no rush, unless you have to go back to work."

"Oh, I'm not workin' tonight, Mr. Gunsmith," she said, putting her hand on his chest and moving it down. "I'm in no rush, either."

"Then call me Clint," he said, "and show me what it's like to be pleasured by the beautiful Melanie."

She gripped his hard cock and said, "You won't be disappointed, Clint."

She got down between his legs and eagerly gobbled down his cock, proceeding to suck it wetly. She was right, he wasn't disappointed. This girl knew how to use her mouth and hands at the same time, and before long he was in danger of exploding into her mouth. But rather than do that he reached down, slid his hands beneath her arms and pulled her up onto him. She knew what he wanted. Moving her hips, his cock slid easily into her slickness. From there she began to ride him, slowly at first, her hands pressed down on his sternum, but then faster and faster as his breath started to come is rasps.

He was fascinated by her chubby breasts bouncing in front of him, while the flesh of her upper arms, belly and thighs jiggled and rippled the whole time. Melanie was the kind of woman who he thought belonged naked and in bed, where she would be any man's dream.

Once again her body was wracked by spasms of pleasure, and she came down on him and stayed there with her eyes wide, grinding now instead of bouncing, and the grinding motion literally yanked his explosion from him. He ejaculated inside of her, and at one point wondered if—and when—it would ever stop. Finally, she collapsed on top of him, covering him with all that wondrous flesh, kissing his face, neck and shoulders while he wrapped his arms around her and held her close to him . . .

***

He watched later as she dressed, felt a sense of loss when most of her flesh was covered by clothes. She came to the bed, then, to kiss him, a long, lingering kiss that would have started things all over again if she hadn't withdrawn in time.

"I'll tell the boss he'll see you tomorrow," she said.

"Melanie," he asked, "did Morehead tell you to sleep with me if you had to, to get me there?"

"He told me to do whatever I had to do," she said, with a lewd smile.

"But . . . you didn't have to," he said. "I had already agreed."

She pressed her index finger to her lips and said, "We don't have to tell him that."

Chapter Five

Clint entered the Immigrant at 8 sharp. There was no line trying to get into the theater. Apparently, the songbird was not singing that night.

He went directly to the bar, where men who must have recognized him from the night before made room.

"Beer," he told Wendell.

The bartender smiled as he set the mug down and said, "Right on time. You can take that with you."

"Okay, where?"

"The boss's office is upstairs," Wendell said. "I'll show you."

"Lead the way," Clint said. "I'm curious about this . . . favor."

As they walked to the stairs, Clint asked, "No theater tonight?"

"No," Wendell said, "she sings 3 times a week."

Clint followed Wendell up the stairs while customers nearby gave them curious glances. At the top Wendell stopped and knocked on a door, then opened it.

"Boss, Clint Adams is here."

From inside a booming voice said, "Send him in, Wendell, send him in!"

"In ya go," Wendell said.

"What about you?" Clint asked.

"I've got the bar to run," Wendell said. "I'll see ya when ya come down."

Clint nodded and entered the room.

A large, florid-faced man in an expensive suit rushed him, grabbed his hand and started pumping it.

"It's so good to meet you, Mr. Adams. Thanks for coming. Can I get you a drink?"

Clint held up the beer mug.

"Of course, of course. Well, please have a seat, then."

The big man rushed around behind his desk and sat down. Clint sat across from him.

"I'm sure you're curious about why I asked you to come here," Morehead said.

"Curious is the word, yes," Clint said.

"I need your help."

"Why my help?" Clint asked. "Can't you hire somebody local? A detective, maybe? Or do you simply need a man like me?"

"This isn't something for a detective," Morehead said. "And I don't need a man *like* you. I need you."

"How did you know I was in town?"

"Wendell told me you were in here the other night, listening to our songbird."

"How did you know what hotel I was in?"

"We asked around," Morehead said, "and found you. So I sent Melanie over to ask you to come and see me, which you've been nice enough to do."

"So now that we've established that," Clint said, "what's this job, or favor, you're asking about?"

"Actually," Morehead said, "it's not for me, it's for someone else. Someone I care about, who has a . . . problem."

"Okay," Clint said, "who is it and what's the problem?"

There was a knock at the door at that point and Morehead said, "Come!"

The door opened and Wendell appeared again.

"She's here, boss."

"Well, let her in, Wendell," Morehead said, "don't leave her waiting in the hall."

"Right," Wendell said.

When the bartender moved aside, a woman entered, and Clint recognized her right way as Sally Songbird. She was not wearing the type of gown she had worn on stage, but a simple dress that covered her from neck to ankles, yet did nothing to hide her womanly charms beneath.

"Sally," Morehead said, coming around the desk and rushing to her side. "My dear, this is Clint Adams. He's the man I told you would be able to help you."

23

Clint could tell from Morehead's tone and attitude that he was in love with the woman.

Sally looked at Clint. From his front seat he had been able to see how beautiful she was, but he hadn't seen her violet eyes. They startled him now.

"Miss Songbird," Clint said, getting to his feet and turning to face her.

"Mr. Adams," she said, in a deep, sultry voice. "That's actually not my real name. Songbird is my stage name."

"I suspected as much," Clint said.

She extended her hand and Clint accepted it readily. They shook all too briefly and then she reclaimed it. He wondered if she stared into the eyes of everyone she shook with?

"Sally, please, have a seat," Morehead said, moving another chair next to Clint's.

"Thank you, Cal."

She sat and he went back around his desk.

"I haven't told Mr. Adams what your problem is, Sally," Morehead said. "I thought I'd save that for you to do."

Sally looked at Clint. Her gaze was very steady—and somewhat chilly.

"I sincerely hope you weren't brought here on false pretenses, Mr. Adams," she said. "Promises of a great fortune for a simple job, perhaps?"

"I don't go looking for jobs, Miss . . ."

"Webster," she said. "My real name is Webster."

". . . Miss Webster. And I'm never looking for a fortune. I'm just here out of simple curiosity."

"Good, good," she said, "I told Cal that I don't want to put any undue pressure on anyone."

"Why don't you tell me what you need done," Clint suggested, "and then we'll just go from there."

Chapter Six

"My mother died recently," Sally said.

"I'm sorry."

"She was elderly and ill. It was time. She lived here in Denver with me."

Clint remained silent, listening.

"She and my father brought me to the West on a wagon train years ago," she said. "In fact, I think it might have been the last wagon train."

"Uh-huh."

"But during the trip my father died, and he was buried along the road. When we got here my mother had to work to support us, and she worked very hard. It was only when I got older and started singing that we did do better."

"I see."

"When I traveled to play theaters all over the country, I took her with me. Then, when she became too ill to go. I started playing theaters closer to home. Like here, at the Immigrant."

"I've been asking her to play here permanently," Morehead said. "But she's got this thing she wants to do before she makes up her mind."

"Okay," Clint said, hoping they were going to get to the point.

"We buried my mother last week," Sally said.

"I'm sorry."

"I don't want you to be sorry, Mr. Adams," Sally said. "I want you to help me bury my father next to her."

"Well, Miss Webster," Clint said, "digging graves isn't exactly my specialty."

"I also don't need you to dig," she said. "What I need is for you to help me find my father."

"Find him?" Clint asked. "Oh wait, you said he died on that wagon train and was buried along the way."

"That's right," she said. "I want to find the gravesite, dig him up, bring him back to Denver and bury him next to my mother."

Clint stared at her, then said, simply, "Oh."

"I'll pay the freight, Mr. Adams," Morehead said. "Whatever you need to make it happen. A buckboard, a casket, anything you think you need."

"Now wait," Clint said. "Your father died years ago, right?"

"Thirty years ago," she said. "I was a small child, but I remember him, and I remember the day he died. And I truly believe that might have been one of the last wagon trains."

Clint knew that wagon train travel peaked in the late 50's, when railroads became prevalent. So she might have been right about that.

"Miss Webster—" he started.

"Sally, please," she said.

"Sally," he said, "there won't be much left of your father if he's dug up. Just some bones . . ."

He trailed off when she lowered her head, but then she raised it and looked at him.

"I understand that, Mr. Adams," she said, "but I want to bring his remains here, to rest next to my mother. Will you help me?"

"It won't be easy to find his gravesite," he told her. "Do you have some idea of where it was?"

"No," she said, "I only know he died sometime after we left Council Bluffs."

Council Bluffs, Iowa was the jumping off place for a lot of wagon trains, but after they left there they could have gone anywhere.

"I'd need to know where the wagon train was headed, what route it took . . . it'll take a long time to get this done, Sally."

"I have all the time in the world, Clint," she said. "There's really no rush."

"Well, that's good," he said, "because I'd want my own horse for the trip, and I left him in Texas."

"I can buy you a new horse," Morehead offered.

"No," Clint said, "for a trip like this I'd want mine."

"Then we can have him brought here," Morehead offered.

"Does this mean you'll do it?" Sally asked.

"I need to think about it, Sally," Clint said, "decide if it really can be done."

"I have some letters my mother wrote to family back East, others that she received in return," Sally said. "Perhaps there'd be something in them to help locate him."

"That'll help," Clint said. "I'd like to see those."

She literally jumped out of her seat.

"I can go to my room and get them now!"

"Your room . . ."

". . . is just down the hall," she finished.

"Oh, I see," He had thought she would be in a hotel. "All right, then—"

"I'll be right back!"

She ran from the office.

"She'll be a few minutes," Morehead said. "Mr. Adams, I don't know if you can tell, but I'm in love with Sally."

"I thought so."

"So I don't have all the time in the world, as she does," he said. "I want to marry her, but she won't agree until her father is buried next to her mother."

"That could be a while, then."

"As I said," he told Clint, "I'll pay the freight on this. Money is no object. And the faster you can get it done, the bigger bonus I'll pay when you return."

"As I said," Clint replied, "I won't be doing this for the money."

"Then why would you do it?" Morehead asked, frowning. "You haven't fallen in love with her already, have you?"

"No, no," Clint said, "nothing like that. It's an interesting problem, that's all. I'd like to see if I could actually do it, find his grave for her."

"Then you *will* be doing it?" he asked.

"Let me read the letters first, see if there's anything helpful in them," Clint suggested. "Then I'll let you know."

Chapter Seven

Sally returned with the letters and anxiously thrust them into Clint's hands.

"When will you let me know?" she asked.

"I'll need some time to go over these," he said, indicating the thick sheaf of letters in his hand.

"Tomorrow, then?"

"I don't—let me see how many I can get through," he said. "I'll come by here tomorrow again, at eight."

"That's perfect," Morehead said. "Sally, we have to give the man time to consider."

"Yes, yes, I know," she said. "I said I have all the time in the world, but I'm also very anxious to get started."

"Well, until tomorrow night, why don't you go through whatever memories you have and see what you can dredge up," Clint suggested. "About Council Bluffs, and possibly the trip."

"I will," she said. "And I'll try to remember stories my mother told me."

Clint stood up.

"That's good."

Sally had not sat back down when she entered, and Morehead got to his feet and came around the desk to shake Clint's hand, again.

"Thank you for this," he said. "For even considering it."

"I'll see you both tomorrow night," Clint said, and left the office.

***

Back downstairs, in the saloon, he returned to the bar, and Wendell wordlessly set him up with another mug of beer.

"So, you gonna be around?" the bartender asked.

"A little longer," Clint said. "But whether I agree to help or not, I'll be gone pretty soon."

"I don't know what they're askin' ya to do," Wendell said, "but the boss is real sweet on the songbird. He'll pay anythin' to keep her happy."

"I got that message," Clint said. He finished his beer. "See you tomorrow night, at eight."

"I'll be here," Wendell said.

Clint nodded and walked out.

***

When he got back to the Denver House the desk clerk immediately began waving at him.

"A telegram came for you, Mr. Adams," the man said, and handed it over.

"Thanks."

Clint took the telegram and the letters to his room, got his boots off, gunbelt hung up and shirt unbuttoned before opening the former.

Talbot Roper was telling him he would be gone longer than he thought, and didn't expect Clint to wait.

Well, he hadn't really planned on seeing his friend before leaving. And now he had a legitimate reason to go, if he decided to help Sally "Songbird" Webster find her father's grave.

He sat and untied the packet of letters. He hoped there would be something in them, because he didn't relish going out to look for the grave with only the woman's memories as a 3-year old to guide him.

He poured himself a glass of water and started reading . . .

***

Many of the letters were written by a woman in love, to her family. The return letters were filled with concern for the woman whose husband was "dragging her" West.

Then the letters became sad and lonely, from a woman whose husband had died.

No matter how much he read, though, Clint couldn't seem to find out how he died. Was it natural causes, a snake bite, or an Indian arrow? Unfortunately, that was a question he was going to have to ask Sally.

There was also nothing about the route they had taken after leaving Council Bluffs. He was going to be stuck with Sally's childhood memories for that.

He set the letters aside and poured another glass of water. It was 3 a.m. and he thought about going out to find a saloon that was still open, but this was Denver, not Tombstone or Dodge.

He refolded the letters and wrapped the twine around them, again. Rather than go searching the streets for a saloon, he got into bed and went to sleep.

***

When he came down to the lobby and into the Denver House diningroom for breakfast, he brought the packet of letters with him. He read them again while eating steak and eggs, and then continued on through several pots of strong coffee. If he thought he had missed something the night before because he was tired, he couldn't find it. He just needed a little something to give them a direction from Council Bluffs.

When he'd had enough coffee, he tied the letters up into a packet again, and thought about Eclipse. He couldn't spend all that time on the trail this task would entail without the big Darley Arabian. He also didn't want to go all the way back to Labyrinth to get the horse, so he was going to have to send a telegram to Rick, telling him to get the animal ready to travel. Then he'd have to turn the task over to Calvin Morehead to make arrangements to bring the horse to Denver, via the railroad.

He could have arranged to meet up with the horse halfway, but that would have meant going South, which didn't make sense, because Council Bluffs was pretty much due East of Denver.

No, bringing the Darley to Denver was the way to go.

That was when he realized that he had already decided to help Sally Webster find her dead father.

Chapter Eight

"Do you think he'll come?" Sally Webster asked Calvin Morehead.

They were having supper, sitting at a large, round table that had been set up in Morehead's room.

"He'll be here," Morehead said. "Don't worry about that."

"What makes you so sure?" she asked.

"Because there's not a man alive who can refuse you anything, Sally."

"Oh, I'm sure that's not true," she said.

"I'm sure it is."

"You're just prejudiced."

"Yes," he said, "I am. I'm glad you know that." He put his fork down, reached across the table and took her hand. "When you get back, I'll have our wedding all planned."

"Oh my God, Cal," she said, "I can't think that far ahead."

"I know." He released her hand. "That's why I'm thinking ahead for both of us."

He picked up the bottle of wine from the table and refilled both their glasses.

"I hope you're right," she said, cutting her veal.

"About what?" he asked. "The Gunsmith, or our wedding?"

"Well," she said, "both."

***

Clint walked into the Immigrant at eight o'clock and space opened up at the bar.

"There you go," Wendell said, putting a beer on the bar.

"Thanks." Clint put the packet of letters down next to it where it was dry, and picked up the beer.

"Where's your boss?"

"In his office," Wendell said, "waitin' for you."

"Is Sally with him?"

"I think so," Wendell said. "They had supper together earlier, but that was in his room."

"So they're together, then?" Clint asked. "I mean, they're a couple."

"Now that's odd," Wendell said. "The boss wants to marry her, but I don't think they've really done anythin' yet except eat together, go to the theater together—maybe she's makin' him wait until after they're married."

"Interesting," Clint said. "Is he that kind of man? I mean, the kind who'll wait on a woman?"

"That's the really odd part," Wendell said. "He's been with every girl who ever worked here. But this one, she's totally different, for some reason. I think he really loves 'er."

"If that's the case," Clint said, "I'd think he'd want to go with her."

"I don't know that part," Wendell said. "I don't know what they're gonna have you do for them, but I do know that he can't leave this place. He never does. He has to keep his eye on everythin' at all times. So whatever he's askin' you to do, it's because he can't do it himself."

"I understand."

"Just remember," Wendell said, "that he loves that girl and plans to marry her."

"Why are you telling me that?"

"Because she's beautiful, and she'll be alone with you at some point," Wendell said. "I'm just warning you not to fall in love with her like everyone else does."

"I don't have any intention of falling in love with her," Clint said. "Can I go up?"

"Sure, go ahead," Wendell said. "But you better knock first, just in case we're wrong about them."

Clint walked across the saloon and up the stairs to Morehead's office, wondered what he would see if he just opened the door and walked in. But he knocked.

"Come on in!"

As he entered, Morehead grinned at him from behind his desk.

"Clint! Have a seat. Great to see you."

Clint sat across from Morehead.

"Is Sally coming?"

"She'll be here in a few minutes," Morehead said. "Before she gets here, have you decided?"

"Yes," he said, "I'm going to help her."

"Good," Morehead said, "and I'm going to do my part. But there's one thing."

"What's that?"

"I'd like somebody to go with you."

"Who?"

"A man I know," Morehead said. "He'd be very helpful, and I'd be paying him."

"To do what?"

"Like I said," Morehead answered. "Help."

"And keep an eye on me," Clint said. "Are you worried about me and Sally?"

"I'm worried about Sally, yes," Morehead said.

"Okay, look," Clint said. "I'm doing this because I'm interested. I haven't done anything like this before. And I'd like to help her. That's it."

"She's beautiful, isn't she?"

"Look, Cal," Clint said, "why did you ask me if you were going to worry?"

"You're right," Morehead said. "When Sally gets here, you can tell her your decision. I'm here with the money."

"And if you want to send someone along with us to help, fine," Clint said. "I have no objection to some extra help. I'll probably need it."

"Good," Morehead said, "fine. I have just the man in mind."

As Clint put the stack of letters on Morehead's desk, the door opened and Sally came in.

"Have a seat, dear," Morehead said. "Clint has something he wants to tell you."

Chapter Nine

"I'll go with you to find your father's grave," Clint said.

"Oh, thank you so much!"

"But I want you to know, even though Mr. Morehead wants to send someone with us, this will be done my way."

"Yes, I understand."

Clint looked at Morehead.

"I also understand," Morehead said. "Don't worry, my man will do what you tell him."

"When can we leave?" Sally asked.

"Not for a while," Clint said. "I have to talk to Mr. Morehead about getting my horse here."

"Just call me Cal, Clint," Morehead said. "He's right, Sally. We have a lot to talk about."

"I don't want to hear all the arrangements," she said. "I just want to know when we're leaving."

"Go back to your room, then," Morehead said. "I'll talk to you later."

Sally looked at Clint.

"Thank you again."

"You can thank me if and when we find the grave," Clint told her.

She nodded and left the office.

"Okay," Morehead said, "tell me where your horse is . . ."

***

Clint told Morehead he would send a telegram to Labyrinth, Texas, instructing them to cooperate in shipping Eclipse to Denver.

"This is going to take the better part of a week to put together," Morehead said. "Are you sure I can't buy you a horse?"

"I'm going to need time to plan this trip, both ways, to outfit us, to meet this fella you want to send with us. You can buy Sally and him horses, but I'm going to need mine."

"Yeah, all right," Morehead said. "I get it. I'll see to it."

"You better send somebody who knows horses, and can bond with them," Clint said. "Eclipse will feel that."

"I know just the guy," Morehead said. "Don't worry."

"I'm not worried about my horse," Clint said, "I'm worried about your guy."

"He knows horses," Morehead assured Clint.

"Well, let me meet him tomorrow and the man you're sending with us."

"Come by at noon," Morehead said, "I'll make sure the doors are open."

Clint stood up.

"I'll be here."

Morehead stood up and stuck out his hand.

"And thank you for doing this," he said. They shook hands. "Stop downstairs. All your drinks are on the house. Wendell knows it."

"I'll do that," Clint said.

***

Clint stopped at the bar and Wendell had a beer in front of him in seconds.

"You on the payroll?" the bartender asked.

"I wouldn't say that," Clint said, "but I'm going to do what I can to help."

"The boss'll be very generous if you do," Wendell said.

"Tell me about him."

"What?"

"Your boss, Morehead," Clint said. "Where's he from?"

"He came here from the East about ten years ago, started buying up property right away."

"When did he open this place?"

"He didn't," Wendell said. "He bought it about 5 years ago, and he's built it up. He bought the building next door and opened the theater."

"He's sending a man to Texas to get my horse and bring him back here," Clint said. "What do you know about his people?"

"He hires the best," Wendell said. "Look at you, look at me. As for your horse, he's probably gonna send Sinclair."

"What can you tell me about him?"

"He knows horses, that's for sure. He'll take good care of yours and get it here safe."

Clint turned his back to the bar and looked for things he hadn't before. He saw there were at least 3 men on duty as security, and 4 girls working the floor.

"There's not a lot of security in a big place like this," Clint said. "I see three."

"There are four," Wendell said, "and they're all good."

Clint started looking for the fourth.

***

Morehead looked up when his door opened and Sally came back in.

"It's done," he told her. "I'll get his horse here as soon as possible, and you can get underway."

"I'm sorry," she said, pacing the room, wringing her hands. "I'm impatient."

"I know you are," Morehead said, "but remember, your father's not going anywhere. He'll still be there when you and the Gunsmith find him."

"I hope so," she said. "It's been such a long time, and there are animals out there."

"I know it," Morehead said, "the two-legged and four-legged kind. That's why I'm glad you're going with the Gunsmith."

"So am I," she said. "He's a legend, and I think I'll feel safe with him."

"You better be safe with him," Morehead said, "that's what I'm paying him for."

Chapter Ten

Clint walked into the Immigrant at 12 noon, found Wendell behind the bar, cleaning it.

"The boss around?" he asked.

"No," the bartender said, "but he told me what's happenin' today. He's got Sinclair comin' in to talk with you, and then somebody else after that."

"Who?"

"I don't know exactly," Wendell said, "but I'll recognize him when he walks in. You want a beer while you wait?"

"Coffee would be better."

"Coffee, comin' up. Grab a table—any one, obviously."

Clint went to a table, took the chairs down from it, and sat. Wendell brought him a cup and a pot of coffee.

"Has the boss told you what I'm going to be doing?" Clint asked.

"Not a word," Wendell said.

"Do you want to know?"

"Honestly? Not really. Not my business."

"Okay, then," Clint said. "Thanks for the coffee. And you might as well bring more cups."

"Right."

He finished one cup, and was pouring another when a man walked in. Wendell simply inclined his head toward Clint.

The man came over, a short, squat man with the scarred hands of someone who worked a lot with horses. As he came closer, Clint could see he was missing parts of two fingers on his left hand.

"Mr. Adams?"

"I guess you're Sinclair."

Clint stood and they shook hands.

"Bites?" Clint asked, indicating the hand.

"What? Oh, the fingers. Oh yeah, two separate horses—bit right through them. Dangers of the profession."

"Have a seat, and some coffee."

"Thanks."

They sat and Clint poured for both of them.

"Mr. Morehead said you'd tell me about the horse."

"Yes, his name's Eclipse. He's Darley Arabian." He went on to tell Sinclair about the horse's personality, his quirks, his needs and his wants.

"Well," Sinclair said, "I'm lookin' forward to meetin' him."

The man immediately fell into Clint's good graces by referring to Eclipse as 'him' and not 'it'.

"When will you be leaving for Texas?" Clint asked.

"Tomorrow mornin'," Sinclair said. "At least, that's what the boss said, if you were satisfied with me."

"Well, I'm satisfied."

"Good," Sinclair said, "because I'm packed and ready to go. I think I can even catch a train tonight."

"You better get going, then," Clint said. "Here." He took an envelope out of his pocket. Inside was a note he had written the night before. "Give this to Rick Hartman when you get there. You'll find him at Rick's Place."

"Rick's Place," Sinclair repeated, accepting the envelope. "I got it."

"And take good care of Eclipse," Clint said.

"I will." Sinclair stood up. "I swear."

"See you when you get back."

Sinclair waved the note, turned and left.

Wendell came over to collect the pot and cups.

"Did it go well?" he asked.

"It went fine," Clint said.

"Good," the bartender said, "I'll pass that on to the boss. You've got about a half an hour before another man walks through that door. You want a beer, this time?"

"Yeah," Clint said, "I'll have a beer."

***

Clint was still working on the beer when a stranger walked in. Wendell looked over at him, then pointed at Clint. The man took a moment, then walked over. He was tall, rangy, in his 40s, wearing a gun on his left hip.

"You're Adams?" he asked. "The Gunsmith?"

"That's right."

"Morehead sent me over," the man said. "I think we're supposed to look each other over."

Clint stood up, extended his hand.

"Clint Adams."

"Rafe Donaldson."

"Do I know that name?" Clint asked, sitting.

"Not like I know yours," Rafe said, also sitting.

"Beer?" Clint asked.

"Definitely."

He signaled to Wendell, who brought over two mugs.

Both men sipped, and then sat back and regarded each other.

"Mr. Morehead told me you'd explain what the job is," Donaldson said.

"I think it's simply to watch my back," Clint said, and then went on to explain the whole thing.

"So find a grave," Donaldson said, "dig it up, and bring the bones back to Denver."

"That's pretty much it."

"And we're doin' this for Morehead's woman," Rafe went on, "that songbird of his?"

"Right again," Clint said.

"Just the three of us?"

"We won't have the problems some of the old wagon trains used to have," Clint said, "so yeah, I think it'll only take the three of us to get it done."

By "problems" Clint pretty much meant Indian or Comanchero attacks along the way. Neither were as active as they were 25 or 30 years before.

"So it's up to you," Clint said. "Are you coming along?"

Rafe Donaldson drank down the remainder of his beer, set the empty mug down with a bang and said, "I wouldn't miss it."

Chapter Eleven

After Donaldson left to get himself packed for the trip, Calvin Morehead came walking down the stairs from the second floor. He stopped at the bar and came over to Clint carrying a beer.

"How did it go?" he asked, sitting next to him.

"It went fine," Clint said. "I'm confident that Sinclair will bring Eclipse here in one piece."

"And Donaldson?"

"I'm still trying to think where I've heard his name," Clint said.

"He's known around here as a man who gets the job done, whatever it is," Morehead said. "It's why I use him."

"I guess that remains to be seen," Clint said. "Where's Sally?"

"She's packing," Morehead said. "It takes women longer. You know that."

"I'll have to see what she's packing," Clint said. "My intention is to travel light."

"For a trip that long?"

"I don't want anything trivial weighing us down."

"Then you'll have to go and see for yourself what she's packing," Morehead said. "Go on up. Her room is the last one at the end of the hall."

"All right," Clint said.

"Come back down when you're finished," Morehead said, "and we'll talk about the finances of the trip."

"Agreed."

***

Clint went up, walked to the end of the hall and knocked on the door.

"Yes?"

"It's Clint Adams."

"Just a minute," she said. "I'm not dressed."

He waited patiently and when she opened the door she was wearing a robe.

"Can I come in?" he asked.

"What for?"

"Cal said you were packing," Clint said. "I need to see what you're planning to take."

"Why?"

"Because we have to travel light," Clint said.

"I'm just taking some clothes."

"Can I look?"

She shrugged.

"Sure, why not?"

He entered, saw the clothing that she had spread out on the bed, apparently with the intention of packing it.

"This is what you were planning to pack?" he asked.

"Some of it," she said, "I—"

"Some?" he repeated. "There's more?"

"I'm just planning to take what I need," she said. "We're going to be on the trail for a long while."

"You're going to need a pair of trousers, and three shirts," Clint said. "That's it."

"What? How can we—"

"You'll wear a shirt for more than a day at a time, and when we get a chance we'll wash them."

"That's disgusting!" she said, appalled. "I can't wear the same clothes two days in a row."

"It'll be more," Clint said, "once we get on the trail."

"And are we going to retrace the trail the wagon train took?"

"Do you remember the route?"

"Well, no . . . I was three."

"I think we'll go straight to Council Bluffs, and try to recreate it from there."

"And how do we get to Council Bluffs?"

"We'll make most of that trip by train," he said.

"And I don't need to wear my clothes more than once on a train, do I?"

"Sally," he said, "I want you to take whatever you can pack into two saddlebags." He held up 2 fingers. "Two."

"That's . . . that's absurd!"

"Remember we said we'd be doing this my way?" he was quick to remind her.

"Okay, just let me pack a carpetbag for the trip to Iowa," she proposed. "Then when we get there, I'll get it down to two saddlebags."

Clint looked down at the clothes on the bed again, then said, "All right."

"Maybe," she said, "by that time I'll . . . get used to the idea."

"I'll leave you to your packing," Clint said, and left.

He was walking down the hall when another door opened and Melanie stepped out, not yet dressed for work. In fact, she was wearing a robe, which stuck to her bountiful body, showing every curve, ripple and nipple.

"Clint," she said. "How nice. Are you just comin' from seein' Sally?"

"Yes, I had to talk to her."

"And was it as pleasurable as talkin' to me?"

"Not even close," he told her, with a smile.

Returning the smile she opened her robe to show him she was naked underneath. Her hard, pink nipples pointed straight out at him, aided by the fact that she was pushing her big breasts at him.

"Wanna come in and talk some more?"

He moved toward her, reached out and allowed her breasts to sit in the palms of his hands, while he flicked her nipples with his thumbs.

"I'd love to Melanie," he said, "but your boss is waiting for me downstairs."

"I say let 'im wait," she said.

He removed his hands and backed away from her while he was still strong enough to.

"Another time," he said. "I'm going to be here in Denver for at least another week."

She closed her robe and said, "That's good to hear. I'll be seein' you, then."

"Count on it," he said, and continued down the hall.

***

Back downstairs Morehead was standing at the bar with Wendell. They both looked up when Clint came down the stairs and approached the bar.

"Any problems?" Morehead said.

"I'm getting some resistance to my ways, already," Clint said. "I need to limit her packing."

"I'll talk to her," Morehead said.

"No, it's all right," Clint said. "I think we got it all worked out."

"She's a stubborn woman," Morehead said.

Wendell put a beer on the bar for him.

"Okay," Clint said, "but last one, until later."

"What are you going to be doing while we're waiting for Sinclair to get back with your horse?" Morehead asked.

Clint sipped his beer, then said, "I guess I'll be doing a lot of planning."

Chapter Twelve

Since Morehead was willing to get Clint anything he needed, he had the man deliver maps to his room at the Denver House Hotel. He poured over them for days, checking all of the established wagon train routes from the days when there were many. In the end he knew he wouldn't be able to make a decision until they were actually there, in Council Bluffs.

During the course of the week, Melanie came to Clint's hotel several times, and they spent the night together. Clint did not find that she was distracting from his plans at all. He reveled in the smell and feel of the woman each time she managed to perform a new trick for him. One night she insisted he take her from behind, got on all fours and presented her majestic butt to him. He proceeded to take her almost brutally, and all she did was love every second of it. He found her lust almost un-quenchable.

Other nights he spent at the Immigrant, drinking at the bar or listening to Sally Songbird, who continued to perform while they waited for Sinclair to arrive with Eclipse.

Finally, on the 6th day, as Clint entered the Immigrant and accepted a beer from Wendell, the bartender told him,

"Boss wants ta see ya as soon as you come in. I think he's got some news for ya."

"Thanks, Wendell."

Clint took the beer with him up to Morehead's office. He knocked and entered, finding the man behind his desk.

"Glad you're here, Clint," Morehead said, "We've got your horse."

"Already?" Clint asked. Even if the steam engine had achieved a speed of 50 miles per hour, Sinclair still would have had to ride from the nearest railhead to Labyrinth, pick up Eclipse and ride back to the railhead leading the big Darley. Whatever the schedule was for the trains, he still expected it to be days before he saw Eclipse. "How did he manage it so fast?"

"That was between him and your friend, Rick Hartman," Morehead said. "Sinclair said Hartman agreed to meet him halfway with your horse in order to get it here sooner."

"Where is he?" Clint asked.

"In a stable not far from here," Morehead said. "If you come by tomorrow morning I'll have Sinclair take you over there. You can examine the animal yourself, to see how it survived the trip."

"I'll be here at 8" Clint said.

"Sinclair will meet you out front," Morehead said. "After you've seen your horse, you can give me some idea when you and Sally and Rafe can get started."

"I'll let you know," Clint said.

"Good," Morehead said. "Then I should be seeing you tomorrow afternoon, or evening."

"Evening," Clint confirmed. "I'll take the day to make sure Eclipse is okay."

"Fine, fine," Morehead said. "I'll pass the news onto Sally."

"How is she?" Clint asked. "She was kind of upset about the packing I told her she could do."

"I think she's dealing with it," Morehead said. "Why don't you have a seat? You can't see your horse 'til tomorrow."

Clint took his beer to a chair and sat.

"Can I tell you anything else?" Morehead asked.

"Yes," Clint said, "tell me more about Rafe Donaldson."

"I told you what I know," Morehead said. "He's done every job I've ever given him."

"Can he use his gun?"

"Oh, yeah," Morehead said, "don't worry about that."

"And do I have to worry about him wanting to try me?"

Morehead hesitated, then said, "Any other time, maybe. But he's working for me, now. This trip you've got no worries. He'll watch your back, and he won't put a bullet in it."

"That's the part I like," Clint said. "What about Sally?"

"What about her? Oh, you mean with a gun? No, she doesn't know one end of a gun from the other. That's going to be your job, and Rafe's."

"Fine," Clint said. "All I need from her is to let me search her memory and do what I say."

"I have to warn you then," Morehead said, "that she can be stubborn, at times."

"How stubborn?"

"She's put her foot down a time or two with me, but," Morehead said, "I think out there on the trail, where she's out of her element, she'll probably do what she's told—most of the time."

Clint muttered, "That's not very encouraging."

Chapter Thirteen

The next morning Clint found Sinclair waiting for him in front of the Immigrant. The two men shook hands.

"That's an amazing horse you've got there," Sinclair said. "Smart as a whip."

"I know it."

"This way," Sinclair said, and Clint followed.

Sinclair led the way down the street and around one corner until they reached a large stable that was virtually behind the Immigrant. The building was very large, taking up most of the block, so it was a long walk the man obviously did not want to make the night before.

"Does Morehead own this?"

"Yeah, he does."

Sinclair opened the doors and they went inside. Eclipse was in a large stall, with plenty of feed, his coat gleaming. He did not look any the worse for wear.

"He looks like he took the trip real well."

"He did," Sinclair said, stroking the Darley Arabian's neck. "I stayed in the stock car with him to make sure there wouldn't be no problems."

"I appreciate that," Clint said.

As he stepped forward, Sinclair moved away to give him room. He also stroked the big horse's neck, saying, "How you doing, big fella? I've got to say, I missed you."

The Darley nodded his head up and down and snorted.

"Yeah, I know," Clint said. "You're mad at me for leaving you so long. But don't worry, we've got a lot of riding to do."

"Startin' when?" Sinclair asked.

"Well, if Sally's ready," Clint said, "and we can find Rafe, and we can get train tickets, probably tomorrow."

"I can see ta all that," Sinclair said. "And I can get this big boy to the train station for ya."

"That sounds good," Clint said, "but I'll go into the Immigrant and have a conversation with Morehead, get things rolling."

"Suits me," Sinclair said. "I'd rather spend all my time takin' care of Eclipse, for as long as I can."

"Okay," Clint said. "I can find my way back to the saloon."

"Good," Sinclair said, "I wanna rub him down a bit more."

"Looks like I'm leaving him in good hands," Clint said, and headed for the door.

"Bang on the front doors loud," Sinclair called out to him. "It's real early for them in there."

"Okay."

Clint went back around the block to the Immigrant's front doors and did as Sinclair suggested, banged his fist on the door until somebody answered.

It was Melanie.

"Are you that anxious to see me?" she asked. She was once again wearing the robe that clung to her.

"I wish that was it," he said, "but I'm here to see your boss."

"That figures," she said. "Come on in. We're havin' coffee."

As he entered, he saw 2 more girls sitting at a table, wearing robes. One smiled at him and one looked annoyed and pulled her robe closed.

"Good-morning, ladies," he said.

They both nodded to him.

"You want some coffee?" Melanie asked.

"Yes," Clint said, "I need some."

"Did you have breakfast?"

"No, I came right over here."

"Well then, sit down and I'll get you some eggs."

"Thanks."

"Here, sit here," she said, pointing to an empty table, rather than putting him with the girls.

He sat down and she came right back out with a pot of coffee and a mug. Behind her, though, came Wendell with a steaming plate of bacon and eggs.

"Bartender and cook?" Clint asked.

"I'm able in the kitchen," Wendell said. "Breakfast is about all I can do."

"Suits me," Clint said. "Thanks. When's the boss coming down?"

"Pretty soon," Wendell said. "He likes to start his day early, but sometimes he'll start it up in his office."

"And Sally?"

"Her?" Melanie said. "The songbird is never up early."

There was a tone in her voice that said she didn't like Sally Songbird very much. It wasn't there the other night when she showed Clint to a seat in the theater.

Melanie sat across from Clint while he ate. He found it hard to concentrate on his bacon with her nipples pointing right at him, but he did the best he could.

"I heard what's goin' on," Melanie said.

"Did you? From who?"

"We've all heard it," she went on. "You're gonna be on the trail for a long time with Sally."

"Yes, I am."

"That means you're gonna need to see me again before you leave," she told him.

"Why's that?"

"You're gonna be feelin' a chill from Sally the whole way," she said. "I'm gonna have to give you somethin' to keep you warm all those lonely nights."

"I'm . . . going to keep that in mind," he promised. He noticed her nipples were poking out beneath the robe even harder.

"Good morning all!" Cal Morehead called out, as he came down the steps.

"'mornin' boss," Wendell called back. "Bacon and eggs?"

"You bet," Morehead said. "I could smell the bacon all the way upstairs. You mind if I join you?" he asked Clint.

"Not at all," Clint said.

"Melanie," Morehead said, as he sat, "why don't you go and join the other girls?"

"Sure, boss."

She looked at Clint, and then moved.

"You better watch out for that one," Morehead said.

"Why's that?"

"Men don't get over her," Morehead said.

"I don't usually have that problem," Clint assured him.

Morehead grinned.

"I wasn't talking about you."

Chapter Fourteen

When Clint met Sally Webster at the train station, she was standing with two carpetbags and a chest at her feet.

"Sally—"

"I know, I know," she said. "I promise you, in Council Bluffs when we're ready to go on the trail, I'll have it down to two saddlebags."

"That'll be interesting," he said.

Coming up behind Sally were Cal Morehead, Sinclair and Rafe Donaldson.

"Ah, you found each other," Morehead said.

"It wasn't hard," Clint said. "I just looked for the prettiest woman on the platform."

The compliment did nothing to make Sally smile.

"I'm just happy we're finally getting underway," she said.

"How's Eclipse?" Clint asked Sinclair.

"Comfortable in the stock car," Sinclair said. "You sure you don't want me to ride with him?"

"He'll be fine," Clint said. "I thank you for your help." They didn't have any other horses on the train. Clint had figured they'd buy mounts for both Sally and Donaldson when they reached their destination.

"All aboard!" a conductor called out.

"Finally!" Sally said.

"Take care of her, Mr. Adams," Morehead said, sticking out his hand.

"I will," Clint said, shaking hands with the man. "Sally?"

She picked up her bags, and Clint reached for the trunk. It was heavy. Rafe Donaldson picked up one end, and they carried it onto the train.

"What the hell is in this?" Clint wondered, aloud.

***

Morehead had paid to get Sally a cabin in the sleeping car. Clint told him not to bother for him and Rafe, they would sit in the passenger car.

They followed Sally to her cabin, carried her chest in and set it down.

She put her bags down and sat on the bunk. The train jerked to a start and began picking up speed. She looked nervous.

"I'll wait in the passenger car," Rafe said, and left them alone.

"Have you ever been on a train before?" Clint asked.

"Yes, but just recently," she said. "When I first came to Denver. But never on a trip this long."

"There's nothing to be nervous about," Clint said. "Trains nowadays make these trips all the time."

"I know, I know," she said.

"Why don't you try to relax, lay down for a while," he said. "I'll come and get you for dinner in the dining car."

"Sure," she said, "okay, thanks."

***

Clint left her cabin and closed the door behind him. From there he went to the passenger car, found Rafe, who was sitting by a window. That suited Clint. He preferred the aisle seat. Even on a train he didn't much like sitting by a window, although he had done it a time or two.

He was just starting to nod off—as much as he ever did, but not so that he couldn't hear what was going on around him—when a woman leading a small boy of about 5 came by, stopped, and then sat across from him and Rafe.

Clint smiled at the boy, who looked shyly away. The mother seemed shy, too, but she stared straight ahead at Clint, until he looked at her, then she shied away. She was a pretty woman, but was probably traveling with her son to see his father, her husband.

However, the boy seemed to overcome his shyness fairly quickly—although he remained seated by his mother and started asking Clint questions about the train, about Indians, about himself and his gun. When he got to the subject of the gun, his mother spoke up.

"Kenny," she said, "stop bothering the men." She included Rafe, even though he and the boy had not interacted, at all.

"But Mom—"

"He's not bothering me," Clint said. "Boys his age are curious."

"Yes, but I don't see any reason for boys his age to start learning about guns," the woman said. "Do you?"

Clint couldn't quite remember the first time he became interested in guns. He did remember the first time he ever picked one up, and how natural it felt in his hand, but he was sure he wasn't as young as this boy at the time.

"Aw, Ma—" the boy stated, again.

"No," Clint said, "your mother's right, Kenny. You're a little young to be learning about guns. Why don't we talk about something else?"

"Like what?" he asked.

"Well, what else interests you?"

"Trains, Indians . . . and guns," the boy said. "We already talked about trains and Indians."

"Yes, we did," Clint said, "but maybe we can think about something else . . ."

***

After another hour of trying to avoid talking about guns, Clint said to Rafe, "I'll get Sally and meet you in the dining car."

"Suits me," Rafe said.

"See you later, Kenny," Clint said to the boy as Rafe got up and started down the aisle.

"See you later, Mister."

"Adams," Clint said, "my name is Clint Adams, Kenny. But you can call me Clint."

"Mama's name is Rosemary!" Kenny called after him, and his mother shushed him.

Clint left the passenger car for the sleeping car, walked to Sally's door and knocked.

"Sally?" he called. "It's Clint."

There was no answer, so he knocked and called again. He was starting to get worried when the door opened. Sally squinted out at him and he knew she had been asleep.

"Sorry to wake you," he said, "but I thought you might want to eat."

"What?" she asked. "Oh, yes, of course . . . just give me a minute to freshen myself."

He nodded, and she closed the door. It was more like 10 minutes, which he spent at the window across from her door, watching the countryside go by.

Chapter Fifteen

Clint and Sally walked to the dining car in silence. He was feeling the chill Melanie had warned him about. Thinking about Melanie reminded him that she had kept her promise. His last night in Denver had been filled with sexual acrobatics, the kind he would remember for a long time—definitely the length of this trip.

In the dining car they passed a table where Kenny and his mother, Rosemary, were sitting.

"Hi, Clint!" Kenny called. "Come with us."

"He can't, Kenny," his mother said. "He has company." Rosemary looked at Clint. "Another time, maybe."

"Sure," he said, "another time."

Sally had continued walking. He caught up to her and they took a table. Clint looked around, didn't see Rafe Donaldson.

"Friends of yours?" she asked.

"I met them earlier today, in the passenger car," he told her. "They're nice people."

"I'm sure."

"Donaldson was supposed to meet us here," he said.

"Then I guess he'll be along."

A middle-aged waiter came over to take their orders. They both chose steak dinners.

"And to drink?" he asked.

"Beer for me," Clint said.

"Do you have wine?" Sally asked.

"Yes, Ma'am."

"A glass of red wine then."

"Coming up."

He went off to get their drinks. Clint looked out the window, this was the only time he ever sat near a window when he was on a speeding train.

"What's our route in the beginning?" Sally asked, when their drinks came.

"We'll be taking the railroad to Des Moines, in Iowa," Clint said. "Then the Muscatine and Oskaloosa to Council Bluffs. From there we'll be on horseback."

"And that's when I have to fit my essentials into two saddlebags," she said.

"That's when you'll have to take stock and decide what your essentials really are."

"Have you traveled with a woman much, Mr. Adams?" she asked.

"Yes," he said, "I know how women pack, but I also know how we're going to have to travel."

"Light," she said.

"Extremely," he said. "We'll need food and water, and some shovels."

"To dig my father up, when we find him."

"Yes."

"And then?" she asked. "A buckboard to take the body?"

Clint hesitated. Should he point out that, if and when they find her father's grave, there may only be bones left? Bones that they'll be able to fit into a saddlebag?

"We'll see when we get there," he told her.

The waiter brought their steaks. At that point the conversation—as sparse as it had been—lagged even more, and they ate, Clint still looking for Donaldson.

"Are you worried about him?" Sally asked.

"Any reason I should be?" he asked. "Is there anything you haven't told me?"

"Like what?" she asked.

"I don't know," he said. "Like maybe something Morehead knows, which is why he sent somebody with us."

"Cal was just trying to be helpful," she said. "I'm looking for my father's grave. There's nothing else to know."

Clint was sitting with his back to Kenny and his mother, which meant that Sally was facing them. She looked past him as they ate, and finally said, "She's an attractive woman."

"Who?"

"The woman with the boy."

"I guess so."

"What I'm saying," she said, "is don't let me stop you."

"Stop me from what?"

"I know your reputation, Mr. Adams," she said. "And Cal warned me about you, and how you are with women."

"And what did he say?"

"That you like women like his saloon girls," she said. "Like that hussy, Melanie."

"Melanie's a nice girl," he said.

"I suppose," she said, "if you like that type of woman."

"And you think that Kenny's mother—her name is Rosemary, by the way—is also that type of woman?"

"Well," Sally said, "she did smile at you—"

"You think because a woman smiles it makes her a hussy?" he asked, cutting her off.

"I'm sorry," she said. "I didn't mean any offense. I'm not very . . . experienced—"

"With people?" he asked.

"I'm just . . . I deal with them on stage," she said. "I don't spend much time with people off stage."

"Except for Cal Morehead."

"Well, he's my boss."

I thought he was more than that."

She lowered her head.

"He thinks he is."

"And he's not?" Clint asked. "He does want to marry you, doesn't he?"

"He does."

"And you don't want to marry him?"

"I can't think about marrying anyone until I have my parents buried next to each other."

"I see."

Clint was starting to wonder if Sally was just using Morehead to fund this recovery trip. And did that mean he was being used, as well?

"Would the lady and gentleman like some dessert?" the waiter asked.

"Sally?"

"I would like some coffee."

"Coffee and pie for me," Clint said. "Peach, if you have it. Apple, if you don't."

"Yes sir, and madam," the waiter said. "Coming right up."

Chapter Sixteen

After they finished eating Sally wanted to go back to her cabin.

"I'll walk you back," Clint offered.

"No," she said, "that's all right. I can find my way. Stay here with your friends."

He wasn't sure what she meant until they stood up and he saw Kenny and his mother were still sitting there. Kenny was working on what looked like a big piece of chocolate cake. Sally walked by them without casting a glance their way. Clint wondered what she had against pretty mothers and their sons?

As she left the dining car, he decided to do what she suggested, and walked down to where the mother and son were.

"Do you mind if I join you?" he asked.

"Not at all," Rosemary said.

"Yay!" Kenny cheered. "I'm havin' cake, Clint. You want some?"

"No thanks, Kenny" he said. "I just had some pie. But I'll have a cup of coffee."

They called the same waiter over and both he and Rosemary ordered coffee.

"What was wrong with your wife?" Rosemary asked.

"That wasn't my wife," he said. "She's just a lady I'm doing a job for."

"Oh, I see," she said. "She's rather . . . chilly, isn't she?"

"You're the second woman to tell me that, and you've never even spoken to her," he said.

"It's in the way she walks," Rosemary said.

"You're very observant," Clint said. "What do you do, Mrs.—"

"Just Rosemary," she said. "I used to be a journalist, until Kenny came along."

"So where are you headed now?"

"Back East," she said. "This may not be the Wild West anymore, but it's still too wild for me to want to raise a boy. I'd rather do it back East."

"Can't say I blame you," he said. He looked at the boy, still shoveling cake into his mouth. "He seems like a smart boy."

"Oh, he is," she said.

"Where's his father?"

"He's not around, anymore," Rosemary said.

That seemed to be all she wanted to say on the subject, so Clint let it go.

The waiter brought their coffee, and a glass of milk for Kenny.

"Where are you headed, Mr. Adams?"

"Please, call me Clint," he said. "Like I said, I'm doing a job for the lady. We're ultimately going to end up in Council Bluffs."

"What's there?"

"The old jumping off point for the wagon trains," he said. "We're trying to track something down."

"Now it was her turn to feel that he had said all he wanted on the subject, so she let it go. He appreciated that. It was Sally's business what they were doing there, and nobody else's.

"Do you have a cabin on the sleeping car?" Clint asked.

"No," she said, "we'll be sleeping sitting up in the passenger car. Actually, Kenny can put his head in my lap."

Clint stared at the pretty brunette's face. She must have been in her early 30s, but her face still had a freshness to it. She could have passed for younger.

"That sounds pretty comfortable to me," he said.

She blushed.

"I'm sorry," he said. "Maybe that was rude."

"No," she said, "it wasn't."

"Hey, Clint," Kenny said, "you gonna sit with us again when we get back to our seat?"

"I sure am, Kenny," he said. "If it's all right with your mother."

"Oh, it'll be fine with her," he said. "She likes ya."

"Kenny!"

"What?" the boy asked. "You said he was a nice man."

"Is that what you said?" Clint asked her.

"Well . . . I might've."

"See?" Kenny said, with a smile.

"Hush now, Kenny," his mother said. "Drink the rest of your milk."

***

When they were finished, they went back to their seats in the passenger car, and Kenny began to fire questions at Clint, again. But when he started asking gun questions, Rosemary stepped in.

"All right, that's enough," she said. "Kenny, lay down here with your head in my lap. Time to get some sleep."

"Aw, Ma—"

"You heard me, young man."

"You better do what your Ma says Kenny," Clint said. "If you don't she might blame me, and then we won't be able to be friends, anymore."

"Are we friends, Clint?" Kenny asked.

"We sure are."

"Yay." He looked at his mother. "Okay, Ma, I'll lie down."

"Good boy."

Kenny stretched out on the seat with his head in his mother's lap.

"Thank you," she whispered to Clint.

"Thank you for allowing us to be friends," Clint said.

They were both surprised to look down and see that the boy had already fallen asleep.

"He's amazing," Clint said.

"Yes, he is," she said, stroking the boy's head.

"Do you want me to keep quiet so you can sleep, too?" Clint asked.

"To tell you the truth, I'm not sleepy at all," she said.

"Neither am I."

That was when Sally came rushing back into the car.

"I need you!" she said.

"Is something wrong?"

She glared at him.

"Definitely!"

Chapter Seventeen

Clint followed Sally back to her cabin.

"What's going on?" he asked.

She waved at him to keep quiet, and reached for her door.

"Look."

As the door opened he saw Rafe Donaldson sitting by the window, apparently looking out.

"Rafe," he said, "what's going—"

"Look closer," she said.

He stepped into the room, got closer, and saw the blood. He was dead, stabbed in the back.

"What the hell—" He turned, closed the door and looked at her. "What took you so long to come and get me?"

"I . . . froze," she said. "I didn't know what to do. I don't know how long I stood here before coming to get you."

"What the hell is going on, Sally?" he demanded. "Why would somebody do this?"

She stared at him with wide eyes.

"How would I know?" she asked.

Clint went back to the body, saw that Donaldson's pockets had been turned out. He searched, found nothing on him. No money.

"It looks like he's been robbed," he said.

"Why'd they put him in here?" she asked.

"They must've seen us get on together," he said. "Somebody stabbed him from behind, then dragged him in here. It can't be a coincidence. They wanted us to find him."

"That doesn't make sense."

"No, it doesn't," Clint said. Unless there *was* something she and Morehead weren't telling him.

"So what do we do now?" she asked.

"We think," he said. "Sit down."

"What? Sit?"

"Across from him," Clint said. "He's not going to hurt you."

"Don't we need to call somebody?" she asked. "A conductor? The law?"

She sat. Clint leaned back against the door, his mind racing. For Donaldson to have been robbed, killed and put in Sally's compartment was too much of a coincidence. Something was going on, which Sally either knew about and wasn't saying, or didn't know anything, at all.

"If we report this, they'll have to stop the train at the next station. We'll be stuck there for a long time while they search the train."

"But won't the killer get off there?"

"If he hasn't jumped off, already," Clint said.

"So we may never know who killed him?" she asked. "Or why?"

"If this isn't just a robbery," he said, "we'll find out later."

"How?"

"When they come after us."

"What?"

"If it's just a robbery," he said, "we'll never know."

"Poor Rafe," she said, staring at the body. "So what do we do?"

Clint looked at the window, briefly considered dumping Donaldson's body out. But if he did that, nobody would ever know what became of him. He would lie out in the wildness forever, his body picked at by scavenging animals. Nobody deserved that.

"Clint?"

"I'm going to move him," he said.

"To where?"

"Someplace where they'll find him at the end of the line, when they unload," he said.

"Where's that?"

"The stock car," Clint said. "I'll cover his body with some hay."

"What if they discover him before we get your horse and leave?" she asked.

"We're not getting off at the end of the line," he said. "By the time they find him, we'll be long gone."

"So . . . how are you going to do that?"

"You're going to keep the conductor busy while I move him," he said. "It's just the next car."

"How do I keep him busy?" she asked.

"Just be a pretty girl."

***

While Sally kept the middle-aged conductor busy in another car, Clint carried Donaldson's body to the stock car. He opened the door, made sure nobody was inside, then dragged the body to a corner and covered it up with hay. When he came out there was still no sign of the conductor. Clint was back in Sally's car when she returned.

"I can't even tell he was here," she said.

"I cleaned the blood as well as I could."

"I want another compartment," she said. "I can't sleep here, knowing what happened."

"You have to," he said. "We don't want anyone else here."

"What if the killer comes back?" she asked. "To kill me, next?"

"Why would he?" Clint asked. "Is there some reason somebody would want to kill you?"

"No."

"Maybe Donaldson was killed by an old enemy," Clint said. "What we have to do is carry on as if nothing happened."

"And when someone starts looking for him?"

"We're the only ones who would be looking for him," Clint said. "Nobody else will even care—not until they find his body in the stock car."

"And if they find it before we can get off the train?"

"We'll just have to act surprised," he said. "Do you know if he had family in Denver?"

"I don't think so," she said, "but I only know that he did jobs for Cal."

"Well, when this is over maybe Morehead can pay to have his body shipped back. As for now, we just keep going as if nothing happened."

She stared at the seat where the body had been.

"This is to get you what you want, Sally," Clint reminded her.

"Yes," she said, "all right. We'll just . . . go on."

Chapter Eighteen

The train made several stops along the way, both to let passengers off and take them on, as well as water stops. Then it went on through the night, until the sun came up and Kenny opened his eyes.

"I'm hungry, Ma," he said.

"So am I," Clint said, once again sitting across from them. "Should we get breakfast?"

"What about your, uh, lady friend?" Rosemary asked.

"If she gets hungry and shows up, she can join us," Clint told her.

"Then let's go and eat."

They stood up and walked to the dining car.

***

Clint was surprised when, even before their food came, Sally appeared in the car. She saw him and walked over.

"Sit and join us," he said to her. "This is Rosemary, and her son, Kenny."

"Hello," Sally said, and sat down, albeit reluctantly.

Clint called the waiter over so he could take Sally's order, and bring all the plates at one time. He and the ladies ordered eggs, while Kenny wanted flapjacks.

"Are you Clint's girlfriend?" Kenny asked.

"Kenny!" his mother scolded. "That's rude."

"It's all right," Sally said. "No, Kenny, I'm not. We're just . . . traveling together."

"That's good," he said. "I want my Ma to be his girl-friend."

"Kenny!" Rosemary squeaked.

That made Sally smile for the first time on the trip, and actually laugh. It seemed to loosen her up, and she and Rosemary began to talk.

When the food came Clint and Kenny chowed down, while Rosemary and Sally didn't let eating interfere with their talking. Clint noticed a warmth about Sally that he had never seen before.

Rosemary was very impressed that Sally was a singer and performed on stage, and Sally was impressed that Rosemary had given up her career as a journalist to concentrate on her son and take him back East.

"You're obviously a fabulous mother," Sally told her.

"Thank you," Rosemary said. "That's so nice of you to say."

"Ma, can we go to the caboose?" Kenny asked. "I wanna look out the back."

"That's kind of dangerous, Kenny," Rosemary said.

"I can take him," Clint said. "He'll be safe with me."

"Yeah, Ma," Kenny said, "I'll be safe with Clint. Can we? Huh? Can we? Please?"

"All right," Rosemary said. "I'll just sit here and talk with Sally some more."

"Sure," Sally said, "let the boys go off together."

"Hurray!" Kenny jumped out of his seat. "Come on, Clint!"

Clint looked at both women and said, "I guess I better get going."

***

Clint and Kenny got to the caboose and Clint crouched down in front of the boy. They'd had to walk through the stock car, so Clint had showed the boy Eclipse, and tried not to look in the corner, where he had hidden Donaldson's body.

"We're going to step outside and you're going to stay real close to me, right?"

"Right."

"Okay, let's go."

Clint opened the door and they stepped outside. Kenny's eyes went wide as he saw the track behind them, and the scenery going by along both sides of the train.

"Wow! This is . . . wow!" The boy didn't have any other words.

So they just stood there and watched.

***

After Clint and Kenny were gone Rosemary asked, "So there's nothing between you and Clint?"

"What? Oh, no," Sally said. "We hardly know each other. And there's a man back in Denver who wants to marry me."

"But do you want to marry him?" Rosemary asked.

"I—I can't think about that," Sally said. "Clint and I have something we have to do before I can give that some serious thought."

Rosemary didn't ask what that something was. She figured if Sally wanted to tell her, she would.

"What about you?" Sally asked.

"What do you mean?" Rosemary asked.

"Are you interested in Clint?"

"My God," Rosemary said, "we just met, and we're on a train."

"That doesn't answer my question," Sally said.

"And I have Kenny . . ."

"It looks like Kenny already loves him," Sally said. "What about his father?"

"He's . . . not around," Rosemary said. "And he never will be."

"Well then," Sally said, "you should take your chance while you have it."

"Meaning?"

"We'll be at our destination soon," Sally said. "Don't waste any more time."

"Are you saying—"

"You know what I'm saying," Sally said, interrupting her.

***

When Clint and Kenny returned to their seats Rosemary stood up and said to Clint, "Could you come with me, please?"

"What about Kenny?" Clint asked.

"Sally's going to sit here with Kenny," she told him.

Clint looked at them, figured Sally would be safe as long as she stayed in the passenger car with all the other people.

"Come on, little man," Sally said. "Come sit by me."

"Rosemary—" Clint said.

She took his hand and led him away.

Chapter Nineteen

"Where are we going?" Clint asked.

"You'll see."

Still holding his hand, she led Clint to the passenger car, and to a compartment, the door of which was unlocked.

"Wait," he said, "whose compartment is this?"

"It's empty," she said, leading him inside.

"But . . . what are we doing here?"

She closed the door, made sure it was locked, and turned to face him.

"I want to be with you," she said. "We may never see each other again when we get off this train. So I want a memory, and I want to give you something to remember."

"Do you mean—"

"Yes, I do." She started to undo the buttons that ran down the front of her dress. "Take off your clothes, Mr. Adams."

"Rosemary—"

She stopped what she was doing and frowned at him.

"Unless, of course," she said, "you don't want me."

"You're a beautiful woman," he said. "Why wouldn't I want you?"

"Then don't worry about whether this is right or wrong," she said. "Let's just do it."

As she peeled the dress down from her shoulders, along with her undergarments, and her small-but-firm round breasts came into view, he thought, yeah, why not?

He also tried not to think that they might have been doing this just feet away from where Rafe Donaldson had been killed.

***

"Where did my mommy and Clint go?" Kenny asked.

"They went for a walk," Sally said, ruffling his hair. "They'll be back."

"Did they go to the caboose?"

"Yes," Sally said, "they went to the caboose."

"That was fun, when Clint took me to the caboose," he said. "My mom's gonna have fun."

"Oh yes," Sally said, "she's going to have a lot of fun."

***

Clint and Rosemary came together in the center of the cabin. He took her into his arms, enjoying the feel of her smooth, hot skin against his. She ran her hands over his shoulders and back while he kissed her neck, and then her mouth, which was hot and avid.

The bunk in the compartment was big enough for one person, but they would make it work. First, they sat while they continued to kiss, their hands busy. Then he again kissed her neck, worked his way over her shoulders and down to her breasts. She had dark brown nipples that had grown hard, and he rolled them in his mouth, making her moan. He bit and sucked them for a good long while, then pushed her down onto her back and continued down her long, lean body until he nestled his face between her legs. She spread them wider for him, and he dove into her with his tongue, making her jerk like she had been struck by lightning.

"Oh, God!" she said, as he started to lick her up and down. "Oh, Jesus, this is so good. Don't stop."

He didn't stop, but he increased the pressure of his tongue and suddenly she became wetter, soaking the lower part of his face. He lapped it up and kept going. He found her clit, flicked it with his tongue, faster and faster, until she gushed again, this time crying out.

"Jesus, how did you get so good at that?" she asked.

"Practice," he said, looking up at her from between her thighs.

"I'll bet," she laughed.

He kissed the soft flesh of her inner thighs, then kissed his way back up over her belly, her breasts, until he was lying atop her, kissing her eager mouth.

She reached between them to grasp his hard cock and said, "Come on, we don't have all day. Put it in!"

He obliged her, lifting his hips, poking the head of his cock up against the moist lips of her pussy, and then gliding right in.

"Eeeeeeee," she went, making a high, keening sound. And then she used a word he had heard Kenny use several times on the back of the caboose. "Wow!"

He began moving in and out of her, reaching beneath her to cup her buttocks. At one point they were moving so hard and fast, slamming up against each other, that they almost fell off the bunk. They both laughed, then went back to kissing, grunting, groaning. It seemed they were making every sound the human mouth could possibly make while he slammed into her, her hips jerking up to meet his every thrust, her eyes alternately opened wide, and shut tight.

Then Clint closed his eyes, grunted, and exploded . . .

***

They dressed quickly. She seemed a bit panicky, now that they had done what they came there to do.

"I have to get back to Kenny."

"He'll be fine with Sally," Clint said.

"I know, it's just . . . I don't do this," she said. "In fact, I've never done this."

"I know you've had sex before," he said.

"Well yes, of course," she said. "I just meant . . . like this. I mean, one time."

"Are you sorry?" he asked, pulling on his boots.

"Oh God, no!" she said, buttoning her dress. "This is what I wanted almost from the first time I saw you and Kenny together. You're so . . . natural with him."

"He's a good kid," Clint said.

"Yes, he is," she said. "And you're a good man."

"You haven't known me very long, Rosemary," he said. "You don't even know who I really am."

She looked at him, leaned over to kiss him, and said, "I may not know who you've been, Clint Adams, but I know who you are right now."

***

Hours later the train pulled to a stop in Des Moines. Clint and Sally were disembarking, while Rosemary and Kenny remained on the train. They still had a long way to go.

"Should I ask where you'll be getting off?" Clint said.

"Probably not," she answered. "Why would you. It's not like you'll be coming to see us."

"Probably not."

They looked over to where Sally was saying goodbye to Kenny. The little boy was hugging her. Kenny came running over to them.

"Will you come and visit us, Clint?" Kenny asked.

"I don't think so Kenny."

He crouched down in front of the boy, who hugged him tightly around the neck. Then Kenny stood back and pressed up against his mom.

"Good bye, Rosemary," Clint said, putting out his hand.

"Good bye, Clint," she said, giving him hers.

He held it briefly, then she withdrew it, put her arm around Kenny.

Rosemary looked at Sally.

"I hope you find what you're looking for."

"Thank you," Sally said.

Rosemary and Kenny got back on the train.

"I hope you two had a good time," Sally said to Clint, as they turned and walked away.

"You set that up?" Clint asked. "I thought she asked you to watch Kenny."

"I offered," Sally said, "and told her that the compartment next to mine was empty."

She smiled, looked away. Clint thought maybe Sally Webster wasn't as cold as he had been warned.

Chapter Twenty

They retrieved Eclipse from the stock car, then found a livery stable where Clint could buy Sally a horse, using money Cal Morehead had given them. Neither of them talked about Rafe Donaldson's body.

"Do you have a preference?" he asked.

"Something gentle."

"You do ride, don't you?" he asked.

"I have ridden," she said, "but not a lot."

Clint found a 6-year-old grey mare that seemed gentle, but solid enough to make the trip.

After they bought a saddle for the horse they went to the general store, and he bought what supplies they needed for the trip.

"What's next?" she asked, when they left with two gunny sacks.

"Back to the train station to get our stuff," Clint said, "and then you'll have to decide what to keep and what to get rid of."

"Get rid of?"

"What else are you going to do with it?"

"I thought we'd leave it somewhere and pick it up later," she said.

"We won't be back this way, Sally," he told her. "We're going to be moving forward from here on."

"B-but . . . I have things I need . . . I want," she said.

"Keep the things you need," he said. "The things you only want will have to go."

***

They found a hotel, left the horses in the livery, where they would pick them up the next day.

Clint got 2 hotel rooms, dragged Sally's chest into hers.

"Start going through your things," he told her. "I'll come by later and get you for supper."

"What are you going to do?" she asked.

"Get some rest," he said. "We'll be on the trail for a while. I want to use a mattress while I can. But I may go out and get a drink, first."

"Don't get drunk using Cal's money," she warned.

"I don't intend to get drunk using anybody's money," he snapped back at her.

She put her hands up in a supplicating gesture.

"I'm sorry," she said. "I didn't mean that." She looked at her trunk. "I'm not looking forward to this."

"I'll see you in a little while," he said.

She nodded. He left the room, went downstairs and out to find a saloon.

***

He had one beer, asked about a good restaurant in town, then went back to the hotel to lie down. After an hour he got up, put his boots back on, and walked down the hall. Sally flung the door open when he knocked.

"This is impossible!" she snapped. "I can't do it."

"What's that?"

"I can't decide what to dispose of and what to take with me," she complained.

"I tell you what," he said. "Let's go out and have something to eat, then come back here and I'll help you."

"How will you decide what I need and what I don't?"

"Who better?" he asked.

"Well . . ." She stepped back and looked around. He peered into the room, saw the contents of her trunk and bags strewn all about the room.

"Looks like an explosion."

She put her hands on her head.

"I'm about exploded in here," she said.

"Steak then?" he asked.

"God, yes," she answered. "I'm starved."

"I asked at the saloon for a good place to eat," he said. "It's not far."

"We're walking?"

"We're walking."

"Well," she said. "Just let me get my shoes on."

Chapter Twenty-One

Their steak dinners were excellent. The bartender in the saloon had sent them to the right place.

"The only place," the waiter told them. "You won't get a decently cooked steak anywhere else in miles."

"That's a bold statement," Clint said. "Des Moines' a pretty big city."

"You go ahead and try and find one, and then you'll see," the man said.

"That doesn't matter," Clint told him. "We won't be back. We're leaving town in the morning."

"Then you will be back," the waiter said.

"How do you figure?"

The older man grinned, showing several gaps.

"We make the best breakfast in the city."

"So we'll be back one more time," Clint said.

"We'll feed you a hearty breakfast to get you on your way," the man promised.

Clint paid the bill, added extra, and they walked back to the hotel.

***

In her room he looked around and shook his head.

"This looks like a daunting task."

"I told you."

He walked around, bent over and picked up a shirt.

"Is this silk?"

"It is."

"Then it goes," he said, tossing it aside. "So does any-thing else made of silk."

"Are you crazy?"

"Silk isn't going to do you any good on horseback, or against the elements."

"So just throw it all away?"

"Or give it way," he said. "I'm sure you can find some girls around here who might want it."

"Do you know how much this all cost me?"

"I don't care," he said. "Get rid of it. Only pack the most durable clothing you have."

"This sounds like it's going to be hell," she said.

"It probably will be," he said. "Do you want to call it off?"

"Before we've even begun?" she asked. "Not likely. All right, then. Everything silk goes. What else?"

"These shoes," he said, picking up a pair. "And these." Another pair.

"Don't tell me, let me guess," she said. "Only pack the most durable pair."

"No," he said. "Wear the most durable pair. You're only going to need one."

"The same pair of shoes the whole way?"

"That's right."

"So when I throw all these things away to make room, what will take their place?"

"You saw what I bought in the general store," he said. "We need room for that."

"Sugar, coffee, canned peaches, beef jerky," she said. "Is that all we're going to eat?"

"You forgot the beans."

"Oh yes," she said, making an unhappy face, "the beans. And the bacon."

"Right."

She shook her head.

"All right," she said. "You can go. I get it. I can do it now."

"Can you?" he asked. "Two saddlebags?"

She nodded.

"Two saddlebags," she agreed.

He went to the door, opened it, then turned.

"One more thing."

"What's that?'

"Can you shoot a gun?"

"I suppose so."

"What's that mean?"

"What's so hard?" she asked, "Just point it and pull the trigger, right?"

"I can see you've got a lot to learn," he said. "But that's okay. We'll have plenty of time."

He left the room, walked back down the hall to his own. He closed the door and made sure it was locked. Once that was done, he stuck the back of a wooden chair under the door knob, anyway. No harm in being safe.

***

He read for a while—*120 Days of Sodom by the Marquis de Sade*—then closed the book. He looked over at the 2 gunny sacks of supplies he had purchased from the general store. They would hang one from each saddle horn, leaving the saddlebags available for their clothes, extra bullets and guns. For now he would let Sally think that her saddlebags would have to hold her clothes, plus some sugar or coffee. He needed her to pack extremely light. He knew she would complain once she realized all their supplies would remain in the sacks, including the coffee pot and pans. But by then it would be too late.

He wondered if she would keep a pair of silk underwear—maybe even wear them—to make herself feel better?

He extinguished the gas lamp on the wall by the door, made his way back to the bed in the dark, and laid down.

Within moments his eyes were used to the dark. He could see the window, and the outline of furniture in the room. He looked up and saw his gun hanging from the bedpost.

It was the last thing he saw before he fell asleep.

Chapter Twenty-Two

He woke the next morning, dressed, made sure his saddlebags were packed, and left the room carrying them and the two gunny sacks. When Sally opened her door to his knock, he expected to see the room still covered in clothes. Instead, it was clean, except for a pile in one corner.

"There!" she said, pointing at them. "Are you happy?"

"Very." Her saddlebags were on the bed, and they looked packed to exploding. But they'd be on her horse, so he let it go. "Grab up your bags and let's go get breakfast."

On the way downstairs she asked, "Are we going to be getting up this early every day?"

"No," he said.

"Good."

"Earlier."

"Oh, God!"

They went to the same restaurant and the waiter greeted them with a smile.

"Got a good breakfast waitin' for ya'll," he said.

"We're ready," Clint said, dropping the saddlebags and gunny sacks onto the floor next to their table.

"Why can't we sit by the window?" Sally asked.

"It makes me too easy a target."

"How can you live that way, always waiting for someone to shoot at you?" she asked.

"You get used to it."

"Really?"

"You have to," he said.

"That's a shame."

The waiter brought them platters of steak and eggs, a basket of fresh biscuits, some butter and honey, and plenty of coffee. Clint knew that no matter what the bill was, he was going to have to pay handsomely for this.

Or, rather, Cal Morehead was.

"Where are we going first?" Sally asked.

"Council Bluffs," Clint said. "Then across the river. From there, you're going to tell me where to go."

"Me?" she asked. "I was three years old."

"Do the best you can," Clint said. "Tell me what you saw, what you heard."

"My God."

"For instance," he said, "where were your parents heading? They must've had a destination in mind."

"My father just said he wanted to go West," Sally said.

"You heard him say that?"

"I think so," she said, "But my mother always told me that, too. In fact, she told me once that she wished my father had a definite place in mind."

"Well," he said, "that's going to make things a little bit harder."

Over breakfast he started to regret having taken this task on. There were plenty of wagon train routes once you left Council Bluffs and crossed the river. Picking the right one was going to be almost impossible, but once they committed to one, they were going to have to keep going.

With the meal over he paid the bill, added enough extra to show how appreciative they were, and then left to walk to the livery for their horses.

"So what will we be doing when we cross the river?" Sally asked him.

"I think we'll start with the most common of the trails," Clint said.

"Which is that?"

"The Oregon," Clint said. "That was a starting point for a lot of people who, later, branched off to the Mormon, California and some other trails."

"Mormon?" she asked.

"Yes, the Mormons came out here and gave birth to towns, like Council Bluffs and Omaha, across the river. In fact, Council Bluffs was founded as Kanesville, and became Council Bluffs around eighteen fifty-two."

"Well, I know the Oregon Trail is famous now," she said, "but I don't know that my father would have chosen it."

"If my only intention was to go West, that's where I'd start," Clint said. "And you said it was soon after you began that your father was killed."

"That's right."

"So there wouldn't have been time for your folks to leave the wagon train and head in a new direction."

"Probably not."

"Do you have any idea just how many days you were on the trail when he died?"

"Mama always said it was almost at the very beginning of the trip."

"Well," he said, "wherever you were headed, it was a long trip, so let's say he died in the first week. That's as far as we'll go with our search."

"And if we don't find him?"

"Then we'll have to try one of the other trails," he said.

When they reached the livery, she put her hand on his arm to stop him before they went in.

"What is it?" he asked.

"I don't think I realized when I got this idea that it would be so hopeless."

111

"It's challenging, Sally," Clint said, "but it's not quite hopeless."

That seemed to mollify her a bit, and they entered the stable.

But he was lying.

This did seem pretty hopeless.

Chapter Twenty-Three

They got their horses saddled, loaded the saddlebags and gunny sacks, and mounted up. As they rode out, they noticed several men had gathered outside the doors, and were blocking the way.

"You the folks who left all them silk things in the hotel?" one man asked.

When they checked out of the hotel, they told the desk clerk about the clothes, and that he could do whatever he wanted with them. Apparently, word had gotten around.

These men were wearing trail clothes and holstered pistols, all seemed to be in their mid to late 30s. Clint had the feeling they weren't there just to see them off.

"We are," Clint said. "What's on your mind?"

"Well," the spokesman said, "we got to wonderin' if yer leavin' that stuff behind, what you got in your saddlebags and them sacks?"

"Beef jerky and beans," Clint said. "You want some?"

The man in the lead laughed, turned to look at his friends. Clint counted 6 men, altogether. This was a potential problem. If these men went for their guns, he was going to have to make sure to shoot the leader, first. Losing their boss usually demoralized men.

"Maybe the pretty lady would like to dismount first and show us what she's got," the man said.

"Are you trying to rob us?" Sally asked.

'Rob' is an ugly word, Ma'am," the man said. "We're just wonderin' what you got, and if you wanna share it."

"I think you men have made a mistake," Sally said.

"Is that right?"

All the men were paying attention to her, now, so Clint let her go on.

"Yes," she said, "all that I had worth anything I left behind in my room."

"And why would you do that?" the leader asked.

"Because my friend here, Clint Adams," she said, "told me to only take what was rugged enough to survive on the trail."

Clint knew she was taking the opportunity to tell the men who he was, in the hopes that would diffuse the situation.

Clint also knew that men like this, once committed, didn't like to back down, even when they found out who he was. In fact, there were times that just spurred them on.

"Adams?" one of the other men said.

"Yes," Sally said.

"Is this your man, Ma'am?" the leader asked.

"We're traveling together," she said. "He's not my man, but he is my protector."

The leader turned and looked at his friends, again. A couple of them seemed nervous, but Clint could see the others were interested. He would leave the nervous ones for last.

"What's your name, friend?" Clint asked.

"Garvin," the man said, "Liam Garvin."

"Irish," Sally said.

"That's right," Garvin said. "What of it."

Sally just shrugged.

"She's too nice to say that you're being stupid," Clint said. "Not giving the Irish a good name."

The man's face flooded with blood.

"Are you others Irish?" Clint asked.

They all shook their heads.

"And was this Liam's idea?"

They all nodded.

"And now that you know who I am," Clint said, "does it seem like such a good one?"

They all looked at each other, but only the 2 nervous looking men shook their heads.

"Looks like two of you are getting smart," Clint said. "Why don't you walk away?"

The 2 looked at each other, then did just that, turned and walked off.

"Now you're down to 4," Clint said.

"It's enough!" Garvin said.

"Now look," Clint said, "we're leaving town. If you make me kill you, I'm going to have to stay and talk to the sheriff. I don't want to do either."

"Too bad," Garvin said. "After we kill ya, we'll just tell the sheriff we killed the Gunsmith. We'll make a name for ourselves."

"I have never understood why men think that killing someone when you have them outnumbered four-to-one is something to brag about."

"Stop talking!" Garvin snapped.

"Okay," Clint said, "but let the girl move away to safety."

"Why not?" Garvin said. "We don't want her dead. We'll have her after we kill you."

"You'll *have* to kill me before that happens," Sally said.

"Sally," Clint said, "Take your horse over there by that tree. That's far enough away."

"Clint, I—"

"I'd prefer not to have to worry about you," Clint said. "It might get me killed."

"Yes," she said, "all right."

She pulled on her reins and took her horse over to the tree Clint had pointed out.

"All right, Liam," Clint said, "let's see how good an Irishman is with that gun."

"Good enough for this," Garvin said.

"Just know I'm going to kill you first," Clint said, "so no matter what happens, you're not going to see it."

Garvin licked his lips.

"You boys still want to go ahead with this foolishness?" Clint asked. "For some silk?"

Chapter Twenty-Four

Liam Garvin drew, and Clint killed him.

The other men froze, with their hands near their guns.

"Don't," Clint said.

They hesitated.

"Right now I only have to explain to the sheriff why I killed one man," Clint said. "Don't make it four."

One of the men stepped forward, raised his hand away from his gun.

"You won't need to explain anything," he said.

"Why not?"

The man was wearing a vest, He drew it aside to reveal a badge on his chest.

"I'm the sheriff."

"Then what were you doing here?" Clint asked.

The man shrugged, let his vest cover the badge, again.

"I'm just temporary until they find someone to take the job permanent," he said. "Liam's idea sounded good . . . at the time."

"Well, obviously it wasn't," Clint said. "So you better get him off the street before you have to explain what happened."

"You heard him," the sheriff said to the others. "And keep your damn hands away from your guns."

They all grabbed the body of Liam Garvin and started to drag him away. Sally came riding back over to Clint.

"In the future," Clint said, "if I want anybody to know who I am, I'll tell them, myself."

"I just thought—"

"Remember we agreed we'd do this my way?" he asked, cutting her off. "That means I do the thinking. Got it?"

"Yes," she said, meekly, "I've got it."

"Then let's go."

They rode away from the livery, and out of Des Moines.

***

It was a 3-day ride from Des Moines to Council Bluffs. It would be a good test for Sally, to see how she would do once they left Council Bluffs and actually started riding the Oregon Trail. If she couldn't take those 3 days, then she would never last that ride.

She spent much of the first night they camped rubbing her rump, but not complaining aloud about the pain from riding. He noticed the second night she never touched her butt.

On the third night they camped just outside the town of Underwood, about 25 miles from Council Bluffs. They were eating bacon and beans which Clint had cooked, and coffee.

"Is your coffee always this strong?" she asked.

"Always," he said. "It's trail coffee. If you were a man, I'd say it puts hair on your chest. Let's just say it'll keep you warm."

"It's Fall," she said. "Why would we have to worry about that?"

"Because we'll be on the plains," he said. "No matter what the season is, the wind can whip up."

She looked up at the moon, then into the fire.

"Don't do that," he said.

"What?"

"Don't ever look directly into the fire," he said. "If something happens, you'll need your night vision."

"What could happen?"

"There are all kinds of predators out here," he said, "both 2 legged and 4."

"You're expecting to be attacked?"

"We were attacked back in Des Moines," he reminded her. "Why not out here?"

"I suppose you're right," she said. "I guess I better stop being so naïve."

"That's a good idea."

She frowned at him.

"You were supposed to put my mind at ease," she scolded.

"I am," he said. "Stop being so naïve and you will be more at ease out here. Just remember to do what I tell you."

"Let's change the subject," she said. "Weren't you going to teach me to shoot?"

"We have plenty of time for that," he said.

"Are we going to buy me a gun?"

"I have an extra for you," he said.

"Is it like yours?"

"No," he said, "it's smaller, easier for you to handle."

"Can I see it?"

He thought a moment.

"Why not?"

He walked to where the horses were picketed, and the saddles were set aside. He dug into his saddlebag and returned to the fire with the little Colt New Line he sometimes used.

"This is thirty-two caliber, but if you put the bullet where it'll do the most harm, it's just as effective as something larger."

"And what's yours?"

He drew his from his holster.

"This is a thirty-eight Peacemaker, also a Colt," he said, then holstered it. "Here." He reached across the fire and handed her the New Line.

"It's not heavy," she said, feeling the weight.

"That's why it's good for you."

"Can I shoot it?"

He reached across the fire again and plucked it from her hand before she had an accident.

"Not in the dark," he said. "We'll start in the morning."

She looked down at her plate, scraped out the last of her beans and bacon and put it in her mouth. Then she picked up her tin coffee cup and held it out to him.

"Can I have some more of that trail coffee?"

Chapter Twenty-Five

For the third day in a row they had beans for breakfast.

"Why didn't you buy any eggs?" she asked.

"Because they wouldn't survive the trip," Clint said. "There's nothing you can do to beans to ruin them."

"Sure there is," she said, looking down at her plate. "Just cook them every day."

"Okay," he said, "when we get to Council Bluffs, we can expand our menu."

"Good." She put her plate down and drained her coffee cup. "Can we shoot now? I don't want to be a bystander the next time we encounter trouble. I'll want to help."

"All right," he said, "but you clean up while I saddle the horses."

"It's a deal."

They stood up and walked away from the fire. Clint chose a tree which had a trunk the width of a man's body.

"Let me see you shoot," he said, handing her the New Line. "Just cock the hammer and squeeze the trigger."

"In one hand, or two?" she asked.

"Whatever's comfortable for you."

She nodded, turned to face the tree and pointed the gun. He noticed she didn't take aim, she simply pointed.

She pulled the trigger, and the bullet smacked into the tree.

"Do that again," he said.

She did.

"You're a natural," he said.

"Shouldn't I aim?" she asked. "Close one eye, or something?"

"No, you shouldn't," he said. "You simply need to point the gun like you were pointing your finger."

He had her fire a few more times, made her unload and load the gun.

"All right," he said, taking it away from her. "That's enough for today."

"Can't I carry it?" she asked.

"No," he said. "Not yet."

"But I want to shoot some more," she said. "It feels good."

"Later today we'll try the rifle," he said. "See how you do with that."

"All right," she said. "That sounds good."

"Now it's time for you to clean up and put out the fire," he said.

"Like we agreed," she said, nodding.

He went over to the horses, put the New Line back in his saddlebag, and then saddled both mounts. He led them over to where the fire had been. She had done a good job of dousing it and scattering the remnants. He watched as she stowed away the coffee pot and the pan.

"Okay," he said. "Let's get started. We should be there before dark."

They mounted up and started riding toward Council Bluffs.

***

They stopped in the afternoon.

"Council Bluffs is over that rise up ahead," he told her.

"So why are we stopping?"

"I want to see you shoot with a rifle," he said. "And I don't want to do it in town."

"All right."

He grabbed his rifle from his saddle, found her another man-sized tree to shoot at.

"This time sight down the barrel," he said. "Put the stock against your shoulder, squeeze the trigger, don't jerk it."

She raised the rifle, did as he said, fired, and missed cleanly.

"Again."

She did it again, and missed.

"Let's get closer."

They moved up a few feet, and she fired a third time. Missed.

"What's wrong?" she asked. "What am I doing wrong?"

"Nothing." He took the rifle from her. "You're a natural with a pistol. And you're terrible with a rifle. Lots of people are."

"So can I carry the pistol when we go into town?"

"No," he said. "That'd be looking for trouble. But once we leave town and start following the Oregon trail, I'll let you carry it."

Her eyes brightened, and they mounted up.

***

Clint had been to Council Bluffs before—but not recently. He had even been there back in the days of the wagon trains. Now, as they rode into town, he saw the growth it had undergone. New streets, new buildings. The law had always been pretty slipshod, so he wondered if that was also new.

"Are we staying?" Sally asked.

"One night," he said. "We'll leave in the morning, after we restock."

"Can I take a bath?"

"Definitely."

"And will that be my last bath for a while?"

"Oh yes," Clint said, "your last proper bath, anyway."

"Meaning?"

"Well, we'll encounter some waterholes along the way that you can use," he said, "but you won't be seeing another bathtub for some time."

"Are you purposely trying to make me change my mind about this?" she asked.

"Not at all," Clint said. "All I've ever tried to do is make you look at this whole thing realistically. We might spend days, weeks on the trail, and never find what you're looking for."

"I understand that, perfectly."

"Then let's get rooms," Clint said, "and that bath."

Chapter Twenty-Six

Clint chose a hotel called the Magnolia Hotel because it had 3 floors and looked like a place that would have rooms available, even in such a busy town.

"And the lady wants a hot bath," he added, when the clerk gave him the two keys for rooms on the second floor.

"There are tubs in the rooms," the clerk said. "I will have the water brought up."

"Thank you," Sally said.

Clint carried the saddlebags up and into Sally's room, dropping them on the bed.

"I'll be back later and we'll get some supper," he said.

"Make sure you give me time for a long bath."

"I'll remember."

He took his saddlebags and the now depleted gunny sacks with him to his own room, set them on the bed. He had an idea occur to him as they rode into town, and preferred to have Sally soaking in a bath than with him when he pursued it.

When he left the room, he took the 2 sacks with him. While pursuing this new idea, he figured he might as well stock up on some supplies.

He left the hotel and found the general store. The clerk who served him was white-haired, in his 60s. While he filled the order, Clint asked questions about the old days.

"Those were the days when I made a lot of money here," the old man said. "Me and my wife had just opened the store, and the wagon trains started rolling in."

"This was the jumping off point for many of them," Clint said.

"And they had to stock up," he said. "All of them." The clerk leaned on the counter with both hands and shook his head. "Those were the days."

"And now?"

"We do all right," he said, "but there are other stores in town, and no more wagon trains."

"So, you must have been here when the last of the wagon trains left," Clint said.

"Oh yeah," he said, "I sold the very last bag of sugar to the last family that shopped here."

"Can you tell me," Clint asked, "where the last wagon train was going?"

"Where most of them were goin'," the clerk said. "California."

"What part of California?"

"Who knows?" the clerk asked. "San Francisco, Sacramento, perhaps Los Angeles. But that didn't really matter."

"Why not?"

"There were families who would leave the train along the way, to settle elsewhere rather than finish the long journey," the clerk said.

"I know," Clint said. "But the remainder of the train was going all the way to California?"

"That was what the wagonmaster said when he came in to shop," the clerk said.

"The wagonmaster," Clint said. "Do you recall his name?"

The clerk thought a moment, then said, "No, I'm afraid I don't. Hang on, I need to go in the back for some of these things."

Clint nodded, and the man went through a door to a back room.

Clint remained at the counter, but from there he could see out the windows. People were walking by in both directions, wagons were doing the same in the street.

"Do you want to take all those things with you?" the clerk said, returning from the back room with his arms full.

"Put everything in these gunny sacks," Clint said. "Then can you deliver it to me at the Magnolia?"

"Sure, but these extra blankets won't fit."

"Just wrap them up then."

The man nodded.

"Is there anyone else in town who was here when the wagon trains were around?"

"Lemme think," the clerk said.

"The sheriff, maybe?"

"Naw," the older man said, "we've had plenty of sheriffs between now and then."

"The mayor?"

"Same thing." He snapped his fingers. "I know. The blacksmith, Jimmy Nash."

"Where can I find him?"

"He's got a foundry on Lincoln Street, all the way at the end," the clerk said.

"What's your name?"

"I'm Felix."

"Can I mention your name to him?" Clint asked. "To get him to talk to me?"

"Sure," Felix said. "Why not? If it'll help you with whatever you're doin'."

"Thank you."

"If ya need anythin' else, just come on back and give a holler," Felix said.

"I will," Clint said. "Thanks, again."

Clint left the store, passing a woman and her daughter on the way in. The woman frowned at him, but the pretty teenage daughter smiled.

***

Clint found the Nash foundry at the end of Lincoln Street, like Felix said he would. If he owned and operated a foundry, chances were that Nash was a bit more than just a blacksmith.

Upon entering, a man looked up from the work he was doing on a piece of metal.

"Help ya?" he asked.

"Yeah," Clint said "Felix sent me. He said you'd be willing to help me."

"With what?"

"Just some questions."

Nash put down the hammer he was holding.

"Come on, then," he said. "We might as well have a drink."

Chapter Twenty-Seven

Nash took Clint into a back room, shuffling as he walked, He was a big man, but he moved like he had ailments. Clint figured he was probably in his 60s, which might account for that.

"Whiskey?" Nash asked.

"Why not?"

The blacksmith got a bottle and two glasses out of a desk drawer, poured and handed one to Clint. He drained his own glass and poured another.

"It's good for what ails me," he explained.

"And what's that?" Clint asked.

"Old age," the man said, "and years of working with a hammer and anvil. Have a seat."

Clint looked around, saw a crate, and sat.

"What's on your mind?" Nash asked.

"History," Clint said.

"Whose?"

"The last wagon train."

"Ah," Nash said. "That was a lot of years ago."

"Apparently you and Felix are the only two around who still remember it."

"That might be right," Nash said. "Whataya wanna know?"

"Where it was going when it left here," Clint said. "And who the wagonmaster was."

"The wagonmaster was a man named Cyrus Elliott," Nash said.

"How do you remember that?"

"I knew him pretty well," Nash said. "He came through here a few times a year."

"That's funny," Clint said. "Felix didn't seem to remember him."

"Well, Felix is older than I am," Nash said. "He's got some ailments of his own, if you know what I mean." Nash tapped the side of his head.

"His memory?"

The blacksmith nodded.

"Ain't what it used ta be."

"Okay, then," Clint said, "Felix said the last wagon train was probably going to California."

"He's probably right about that," Nash said. "Cyrus usually took his people that far."

"Where is Cyrus now?"

"Damned if I know," Nash said. "He's gotta be pretty old, if he's even still alive. I ain't seen him in years."

Clint sipped his whiskey and set the glass down.

"What's your interest in the last wagon train?" Nash asked.

"I'm looking for a man who died on it," Clint said. "He was buried somewhere along the way, and I'm trying to find his grave site."

"Jesus Christ, man," Nash said. "That's gonna be impossible."

"Damn near, I guess," Clint said. "But I'm going to try."

"What was the man's name?"

That was the moment Clint realized he didn't know Sally's father's full name.

"Webster," Clint said. "His name was Webster."

Nash shook his head.

"Don't know it."

Clint stood up.

"I guess I'll just have to make do with what I've got," Clint said. "Thanks for your time."

"No problem," Jimmy Nash said.

They walked back into the shop together, where Nash picked up his hammer. Clint kept walking and went out the door.

***

Figuring he had given Sally enough time to soak in her bath, Clint went to the second floor of the Magnolia Hotel and knocked on her door.

"Who is it?" she called out.

"It's Clint."

"Oh, come on in. The door's unlocked."

Clint opened the door and went inside. He looked around, didn't see Sally anywhere. But he knew from his own room that the bathtub was in a small room of its own. She must still be in the bath.

"I thought you'd be done," he called out. "Why don't I go downstairs and wait?"

"You don't have to do that," she called back. "In fact, I need some help in here. I can't get out of the tub."

"What?"

"Can you come in here and help me?"

Clint looked at the closed door.

"You want me to come in there?"

"That's right."

What did she have on her mind? Or was she really in some kind of distress.

"I've been waiting for you to show up," she called out. "I've been stuck here for a while."

He walked to the door.

"Sally—"

"Oh, come on, Clint," she said. "I need you in here."

"Okay," he said, "I'm coming in."

He opened the door and stepped inside. The room was roughly the size of a 6x6 jail cell, with the bathtub set right in the center.

Sally stared at him from the water, her hair plastered to her head, her body submerged.

"What's going on, Sally?" he asked. "What's the problem?"

"Did I say there was a problem?" she asked.

"You said—"

"—that I needed you in here." Abruptly she stood up, the water running down her naked body, sluicing down her small breasts, dripping from her hard nipples. "And I do!"

Chapter Twenty-Eight

Clint was struck dumb for a moment, but recovered quickly.

"Sally," he said, "what are you doing?"

"What does it look like I'm doing?" she asked, putting her hand out to hm. "I need help getting out of the tub, or I might slip and fall."

Clint decided to go along with her and see how far she was going to push this.

He stepped to the tub and took her hand. Gracefully, she stepped out and stood next to him, tall and slender.

"A towel, please?" she asked.

He reached for a towel and started to hand it to her, but she turned.

"Can you dry my back, please?"

"Whatever you say."

He patted her back with the towel, then started to rub. He moved down, to her lower back, and then to the firm globes of her ass. She backed up and pressed herself against him.

"My legs?"

He ran the towel up and down one leg, and then the other. She stepped away from him, leaving him slightly damp, and turned to face him.

"My front, please?"

He dried her shoulders, then her breasts. He could feel her nipples through the cloth. Suddenly, she spread her legs further, and he knew what she wanted.

"Sally—"

"Just do it."

He ran the towel down over her belly, then dried her inner thighs before pressing the cloth to her pubic bush, which glistened with water drops. He dried it, then pressed harder so that she caught her breath as he rubbed her pussy lips up and down.

"That's enough," she said, closing her eyes.

"We're done?" he asked, tossing the towel away.

"No," she said, stepping close to him and putting her arms around his neck, "we're moving to the bed."

"Sally—"

"You didn't turn Rosemary away, did you?" she asked.

"Well, no—"

"She told me what it was like to be with you," she said. "Also told me I'd be foolish not to do it myself." She shrugged. "I think this is my last chance, before we get on the trail."

"Sally, what about Cal," Clint asked. "He wants to marry you when you get back."

"So?" she said. "He knows I'm not a virgin. Why would he have to know anything happened between us?"

The look in her eyes, the glisten on her lips, the heat from her body, were all working against his better judgment.

"Just this one time?" he asked.

"Just this once."

She pulled on his neck before he could come up with any more excuses, and kissed him. Her mouth was tentative at first, but then it became more insistent. She opened her mouth and pushed her tongue into his, pressed her naked body against him. Abruptly, he broke the kiss, lifted her into his arms and carried her to the bed.

***

Jimmy Nash looked up as the door to his shop opened. Felix Walker, who owned the general store, came in. Nash put his hammer down.

"Whiskey?" he asked.

"Definitely."

The 2 old men went back to the office where Nash poured 2 glasses.

"Was he here?" Felix asked.

"Yeah, he was."

"What did you tell 'im?"

"Not much," Nash said.

"About Cyrus?"

"Yes."

"Do you know where Cyrus is now?" Felix asked.

"In the ground."

Nash poured 2 more glasses full.

"What do we do now?" Felix asked.

"Well," Nash said, "we're too goddamned old to do anything ourselves."

The 2 men thought for a moment.

"So we hire somebody," Felix said.

"Yeah."

"Who?"

Nash rubbed his jaw.

"Somebody who's not afraid," he said. "Do we know who this fella is?"

"I checked at the Magnolia Hotel," Felix said. "It's Clint Adams. At least, he's checked in that way."

"The goddamned Gunsmith?" Nash said.

Felix nodded.

"Jesus!"

"So we're gonna have to hire more than one man," Felix pointed out.

"When are they leavin'?" Nash asked.

"Tomorrow."

"Goddamnit," the blacksmith said. "We gotta act fast."

"You got somebody in mind?" Felix asked.

"I do," Nash said, "and he'll do it, but he's gonna have to find himself some men to back his play."

"Can you get ahold of him today?"

"I'm sure as hell gonna try!" Jimmy Nash said.

Chapter Twenty-Nine

Clint laid Sally gently on the bed.

His initial impression of Sally "Songbird" Webster was that she was a delicate creature. Now, seeing her naked, he realized there was nothing delicate about her. Though long and lean, she was a solidly built girl. For just a moment he rethought having her along on this trek, and thought that she probably wouldn't be as helpless as he originally thought.

Lying on her back she looked up at him and spread her legs. He ran his hands over her breasts, squeezed the nipples, glided his palms down over her belly until he had one hand between her legs. He found her wet and ready there, and not from the bath.

He slid one fingertip along her wet slit and she caught her breath. When he slid a finger inside of her, she closed her eyes, bit her lip and moaned.

He removed his hands from her and took the time to undress himself, hanging the gunbelt nearby. When his hard cock came into view, her eyes widened and she reached for it.

"Rosemary didn't lie," she said, as she stroked him.

"You talked about—"

"Everything," she told him. "We talked about everything."

Just for a moment he felt embarrassed, but it only lasted a moment because her hand became more insistent. She began to vigorously pump his cock, causing it to swell even more, and with her other hand she stroked his thighs and fondled his testicles.

He got onto the bed with her so he could gather her into his arms and kiss her again. Their legs entwined as their mouths fused together, so that they were joined in more ways than one.

***

Jimmy Nash heard the door to his shop open again. He thought Felix might be coming back. Hoped it wasn't the Gunsmith returning, but when he stepped out of his back room he saw it was Nathaniel Banks.

"I heard you were lookin' for me," Nate Banks said.

He was a tall man in his 30s, with a holstered gun on his left hip. It was known that when Nate drew his gun, he usually fired it, and when he fired it, he hit what he was shooting at. And yet he was not known as a fast gun.

"Whiskey?" Nash asked.

"No, thanks," Nate said.

"Well I want one," Nash said. "Come on in the back."

Nate followed the older man into his office, watched while he poured himself a glass of whiskey.

"Whataya need, Jimmy?"

"You know who the Gunsmith is?"

"Sure," Nate said. "Old West legend. He's dead, isn't he?"

"No," Nash said, "he's in town."

"Really? You tell the sheriff?"

"It ain't my job to tell the sheriff," Nash said. "Let him find out on his own."

"So what do you need me for?"

"Adams is here lookin' for the last wagon train."

"What for?"

"Some fella died on that train, got buried along the way," Nash said. "He's tryin' to find that fella's grave."

"Again," Nate said, "why?"

"I don't know why," Nash said. "I only know that he is. That's all I care about."

"Don't make me ask again," Nate said.

"Look," Nash said, "have a seat and I'll tell you what I'd like you to do, and how much I'm gonna pay you."

Nate sat down.

"Can we start with the last part first?"

Nate Banks' listened intently once Jimmy Nash told him how much was involved.

"So you're not going to pay me up front," Nate said, when Nash was done.

"No," Nash said, "you get yours when we get ours."

"So let me get this straight," Nate said. "You want me to follow him until he finds what he's looking for, and then take it away from him?"

"That's right," Nash said, "but don't follow him, track him. If you follow too close he's gonna see you."

"Is he gonna be alone?"

"I don't know," Nash said. "We'll know that when he leaves tomorrow mornin'."

"So you don't know how many men I might need to get this done," Nate said.

"Well," Nash said, "he is the Gunsmith, right?"

"Right," Nate said. "I've got a few guys I can use, but who's paying them?"

"You are," Nash said, "out of your end."

"I'm not sure I like that," Nate said.

"Then I can get somebody else."

"No," Nate said, "I'll do it." He stood up. "You want to know who I'll be using?"

"No," Nash said. "I trust you."

Nate started out of the room, but stopped at the door and turned back.

"You know I'm not a fast gun, right?"

"Right."

"So I don't have any desire to go up against this guy, or test myself."

"Look," Nash said, "however you decide to get this done is fine with me. Just get it done."

"Got it."

Nate Banks left.

Chapter Thirty

Clint coupling with Rosemary had been hasty. But since Rosemary had thought enough of it to relate it to Sally, he decided to take his time with her, and give her more than Rosemary had received.

So he went slowly, using his hands, fingers, mouth, tongue and, at one point, even the tip of his nose. It was all designed to bring her to the brink, and then back off. Before long, she was writhing on the bed, her body begging for release, but with her desperately wanting it *not* to end.

She may not have been a virgin—and he soon discovered that was true—but neither was she very experienced. At one point, when he slid down between her thighs to press his mouth to her pussy, she suddenly clamped her thighs shut.

"What are you doing?" she asked.

"Making love to you. I thought you said you weren't a virgin."

"I'm not," she said, "I've just . . . nobody's ever done that to me before."

Clint usually ran into women like this who, in their 30s, had only made love in one or two ways.

"It's all right," he said, putting his hands on her thighs and gently spreading them, "let me show you."

When he touched her with his tongue and lips, she sighed and allowed her legs to fall open . . .

***

Jimmy Nash reached the general store just as Felix Walker was getting ready to close up.

"Lock that door!" Felix snapped.

Nash did so, then turned to look at his old comrade.

"Whiskey?" he asked.

"In the back."

They both went to the back room, where this time it was Felix pouring the drinks.

"I got Banks," Nash told him.

"He agreed?"

Nash nodded.

"How much?"

"An equal share."

"Really?"

"But he pays his men out of his end," Nash went on.

"I guess that's fair."

"Look," Nash said, "this has been a long time comin', Felix. We gotta do what we gotta do."

"I get it," Felix said. "Did you tell him who he's going up against?"

"I did," Nash said.

"And he still agreed?"

"He'll have some men with him," Nash pointed out.

"How many?"

"Why does that matter?" Nash asked. "He's gonna do what we want. That's all that counts."

"And if Adams finds what he's lookin' for, and Banks takes it away from him," Felix said, "you really think he's gonna come back?"

"He'll come back."

"How do you know?"

"I trust him," Nash said.

"Why?"

"Because I know 'im," Nash said. "He's not that way. When he agrees to do somethin', he does it."

"Let's hope you're right," Felix said.

"I better be," Nash said. "You and me, our asses are too old for the saddle."

Nash looked at his empty glass.

"You wanna get drunk?" he asked Felix.

"Hell, no," Felix said. "I got work to do. Go get drunk in a saloon. Or, better yet, go home."

"Yeah," Nash said, "I'll go home."

"But try to get up in the mornin' and see what's goin' on, huh?" Felix asked his friend. "I'd like to know for sure that Banks is on the job."

"He'll be on the job," Nash said, heading for the door.

"Just make sure, huh?" Felix called after him.

Nash waved without turning.

***

"Omigod!" Sally breathed.

Clint was lying next to her.

"That was . . . is it always like that?"

"Hopefully."

She covered her face with her hands and moaned out loud.

"What about you and Cal?" he asked. "Haven't you been to bed?"

She removed her hands from her face, put them at her sides.

"No," she said. "I've managed to . . . stave him off, so far."

"So maybe it'll be like this with him."

"I doubt it," she said. "He's a very . . . simple man. In fact, one of the other girls told me he just ruts, then rolls off and goes to sleep."

"One of the other girls?"

"Not Melanie," she assured him.

"Oh, that wouldn't matter to me," he replied.

"I thought you liked her?"

"I did," he said. "I do, but I doubt I'll ever see her again."

They fell quiet for a few minutes before she spoke again.

"So when this is done, we'll never see each other again," she said.

"Probably not."

She reached out, touched his belly, ran her hand down further until she was stroking his cock, bringing it to life, again.

"I thought you weren't very experienced," he said. "Your hand sure knows what it's doing."

"So does my mouth," she said. "Let me show you."

Chapter Thirty-One

Clint had managed to get back to his own room and catch some sleep before the sun came up. He knocked on Sally's door and she was smiling when she opened it, her saddlebags over her shoulder.

"Breakfast?" she asked.

"Yes," he said, "and our supplies should be waiting downstairs."

"More than beans?" she asked.

"I hope so."

They went down and found their gunny sacks filled to capacity, waiting at the desk. They checked out and left the hotel, carried their load to a nearby café where they had a large breakfast Clint hoped would hold them for most of the day.

That done, they headed for the livery, saddled their horses, loaded them down with saddlebags and gunny sacks, and mounted up.

"I noticed they have a telegraph office here," Sally said. "Do you think we should let Cal know what's going on before we leave?"

"There's nothing he can do from where he is."

"That's true."

"No, we're just going to cross the river and hope that we're traveling the same route as the last wagon train."

"Looking for a single grave," she added.

"Yes," he said. "Since you mentioned it, do you have any recollection of what kind of marker was put on it?"

"You mean was it large enough to have lasted all these years?" she asked.

"That's what I meant, yes."

"All I remember was that it was more than just a cross made up of branches," she said. "My mother said she insisted that it be something people would see."

"Well, let's hope that's what it was."

***

Clint and Sally rode past the general store on their way out of town. Inside, staring out the window, were both Felix Walker and Jimmy Nash.

"Just him and a girl," Felix said.

"Yeah," Nash said. "Wonder what the girl's got to do with this?"

"Who cares?" Felix asked. "Where the hell is Banks?"

"He'll be along," Nash said. "I told him not to follow too close behind."

"Then he better have somebody with him who can track," Felix said.

Nash stepped away from the window.

"Don't worry," he said. "Nate Banks knows his job."

"He better."

"And we better open our shops," Jimmy Nash said. "We don't want nobody wondering why we're closed."

***

From the roof of the Magnolia Hotel, Nathaniel Banks watched as Clint Adams and a girl rode out of town.

"That him?" Cassius Pride asked.

"That's him."

"That's a helluva horse he's ridin'," Cass said. "How we gonna catch him?"

"We're not going to try to catch him," Nate said. "We're just going to track him."

"And that's why we got the Indian with us?" Cass looked over at Charlie One-Feather, who returned the look with a baleful stare of his own.

"That's why." Nate moved away from the edge of the roof. "Come on, let's get to our horses and the others."

As they made their way down from the roof Cass asked, "You think the Gunsmith ain't gonna notice 5 of us trailin' him?"

"We'll stay back far enough so he doesn't see our dust," Nate told him.

Behind the hotel were 2 other men, holding 5 horses. Banks, Cass and One-Feather all mounted up.

"What now?" Cass asked.

Nate nodded at One-Feather, who gave his horse his heels and rode off.

"He's goin' without us?" Cass asked.

"He's going ahead of us," Nate said, "and he'll leave a trail."

"And what do we do?" Cass asked.

"Let's go get a beer," Nate said.

***

Clint and Sally crossed the Missouri and stopped on the other side.

"Omaha's that way," he said, "and the Oregon Trail is that way."

"Are we going to follow the Trail?"

"That's what we're going to do," Clint said, "at least for a while. At certain points it branches off onto other trails, but we'll make those decisions when we come to them."

She looked around, then back at him and asked, "How about that gun?"

"What?"

"You said when we got onto the trail, you'd let me carry that gun, remember?"

"I did say that, didn't I?"

"Yes, you did."

This time he looked around them.

"I think we can put that off for a while," he said.

"How long?"

"When we camp," he said. "We'll go through another lesson or two, and then I'll let you carry it."

"Clint," Sally said, "don't trust me with a gun?"

"Let's just keep moving," he said, "and talk about this later. I want to put some distance between us and Council Bluffs."

"Why?" she asked. "Are you thinking that whoever killed Rafe Donaldson is behind us?"

"Well," Clint replied, "I'm sure as hell hoping they're not ahead of us."

Chapter Thirty-Two

Clint kept checking their back trail, but never saw a sign of dust to indicate they were being followed.

"Can't we go faster?" Sally asked.

"Why?" Clint asked. "We're not in a hurry to get anywhere. We need to travel at the same speed the wagon train was going. That way we won't overlook anything along the way."

"But I thought we'd see remnants along the trail," she said. "Broken wheels, discarded furniture—my mother once told me that people were always leaving beds, chests, and tables behind when it became necessary for them to lighten the loads in their wagons."

"That's right," Clint said. "People often packed way more than they needed."

"You mean like I did?"

"For you it was too many of the wrong items of clothing," he said. "For the people on the wagon trains it was too many heavy items. They brought them all this way from their homes, just to have to leave them behind."

"So where are they?"

"That was years ago," Clint said. "whatever the Indians or two-legged scavengers didn't take would have turned to dust, by now."

"Then why did you agree to this, if you don't think we'll find anything? The money?"

"Money's not an issue for me," he said. "I figured you had to at least try this if you were going to get on with your life."

"So you're doing this for me?" she asked. "You didn't even know me when you agreed."

"Let's just say I was in between adventures."

"Oh, is that what this is to you?" she asked. "An adventure?"

"Well, I was going to say I was in between jobs, but that's not accurate either. I guess I was just looking for something."

Truthfully, if Talbot Roper had not been out of town when he arrived in Denver, he wouldn't have been in Nebraska with Sally, hunting down the last wagon train to find her father's grave.

"So I guess, yes, I'd say this was an adventure for me. If that offends you, then I'm sorry."

"Hey," she said, "if you want to describe your life as a series of adventures, be my guest."

"My life is what it is," he said, "I don't try to define it, or describe it."

"So if we're not looking for the remnants left behind by the members of a wagon train," she asked, "what *are* we looking for?"

"A likely place for a grave," Clint said. "I don't suppose the wagon trains stopped where they were when someone died and simply dug a hole."

"No," she said, "my mother said they searched for a good place to bury my father."

"Then there you go," he said. "Now we're looking for more than just a hole in the ground."

***

They stopped to rest the horses—primarily Sally's horse—and Clint took the opportunity to let her shoot again.

She fired 3 three times and hit it all 3. He then went through unloading and reloading the gun, and putting it into her waistband where it would be the most comfortable, and least dangerous.

"Can I get a holster?" she asked.

"Maybe somewhere along the way," he agreed.

He tried her with a rifle again, but no matter what he told her, she was awful. He finally gave up.

"Here," he said, handing her the Colt New Line. "You've earned it."

She held the gun in both hands, stared at it, then slid it into her belt.

"I feel different," she said.

"Well, don't," he told her. "It's just a gun, a tool. And one we try not to use."

"Really?" she asked. "With your reputation?"

"I never draw my gun unless I'm going to use it," he said, "and I never use it unless I have to. Reputation or not."

"I'm sorry," she said. "I didn't mean any offense."

"Let's mount up and get moving," he said. "We have a lot of daylight left, and I want to use it all."

***

They stopped along the way to check likely locations for a grave: a gulley, a hill, a field. They actually did find several graves, but Clint could tell immediately that they were recent.

"And this one," he said, at one, "is too small, probably a child or an animal."

"People bury animals?"

"Usually dogs," he said. "People with dogs come to love them as if they were a child."

"That sounds . . . weird to me. An animal is an animal. It's not a person."

Clint didn't want to argue the point with her, because then he would have to deal with the way he felt about Duke, his old black gelding, and Eclipse. He never thought of either one of them as animals. They were his partners.

"Let's keep moving."

***

They finally camped at the end of the first day, and divvied up their chores. Clint took care of the horses while Sally collected wood and started the fire. But it was Clint who made the coffee and did the cooking.

"Bacon and beans?" she asked, when he handed her a plate.

"We'll try something new another night," he said. "I've got the makings for some trail biscuits. Right now I'm too hungry to make a fuss."

"I know," she said, "I'm starving. But on the bright side, my ass doesn't hurt. I think I'm getting used to the saddle."

"And now you can get used to something else," he said.

"Like what?"

"Standing watch."

Chapter Thirty-Three

He told her she would be taking the first watch and to wake him after 4 hours.

"What am I watching for?" she asked.

"You're not only watching, you're listening," he replied. "For anything. If you think you hear an animal, or a man, approaching the camp, wake me up right away."

"Should I sit with my gun in my hand?" she asked.

"No, but you can keep my rifle across your knees," he said. "If you have to squeeze off a shot to wake me, do it."

"And we'll be doing this every night?" she asked.

"Every night that we're out here," he said.

"Why didn't we do that when we were between Des Moines and Council Bluffs?" she asked.

"I didn't feel it was necessary then," he said. "But the more I think about it, the more I think we should have."

"So you do think that Donaldson was killed because of this?" she asked.

"It's just too much of a coincidence that he was killed and put in your compartment," Clint said. "It had to be some kind of message, or warning."

"Saying what?"

"That they're coming."

"Who?"

"I don't know," Clint said, "but I have a feeling we're going to find out."

"Well . . . all right, then. Four hours?"

"Right," he said, "and remember, don't look into the fire."

"My night vision," she said. "Right."

"And listen to Eclipse.'"

"What? Listen to your horse?"

"Yea," Clint said. "If he acts up, it's likely because someone or something is coming close to the camp."

"The horse does that?"

"Yes, he does," Clint said. "You'll both be on watch."

He covered himself up in his bedroll as she sat down by the fire.

"And make sure there's coffee when I wake up," he called out.

"Right."

He laid there awake for a while, watching her. She jerked her head up a few times, probably thinking she saw or heard something. Once she looked over at Eclipse. But eventually, she settled down, and he was able to close his eyes for a while . . .

***

When she woke him, he was actually already awake, but he remained there and waited for her to rouse him.

"Clint?" she touched his shoulder.

"Hmm? What?"

"I hate to wake you, but it's your turn."

"Fine." He rolled out and stood up, took the rifle from her. "Go ahead and get some sleep."

"Thank you."

She rolled herself up in her own bedroll, said, "There's a full pot of coffee," and was asleep before he could get to the fire.

***

In the morning he tried to introduce something new into the bacon and beans by breaking up some beef jerky and mixing it in. It turned into some sort of hash, which she downed without complaint.

"You looked rested," he commented.

She looked back at him across the fire with bright eyes.

"I am," she said. "I feel great. I think maybe it's because I'm contributing by standing watch. Did I do a good job?"

"Well," he said, "we still have our horses, and we're still alive, so I'd say yes."

She cleaned up, doused the fire and stowed the gear while he saddled the horses.

"I'm hoping we'll find something today," she said.

"Maybe we will," Clint said, although he didn't hold out much hope. It was only their second day on the trail.

***

Clint was not surprised at how many graves they found along the way, but there were only 2 where he pressed the shovels into play.

One turned out to be a mass grave, with a collection of bones from several different bodies.

The second looked promising, but when he reached the bones, wrapped in a tattered blanket, Sally said, "That's not him."

"How can you tell?"

"Mama said she buried him with a Bible."

"That book could be long gone, by now, turned to dust," he said.

"But it had a leather cover," she said. "That would last longer, wouldn't it?"

"I suppose it would," he said.

"So that's not him."

They continued on. Clint wondered if and when they found a grave that she believed was her father's, whose bones would they actually be taking back to Denver? And did it matter, as long as she thought they were her father's bones?

***

They spent 2 more days riding and digging, and when they camped on the 3rd night, Sally was no longer so bright-eyed.

"This seems hopeless," she said.

"Let's give it a few more days before we start thinking that," he said. "Your mother seemed sure your father died during the first week. Let's give it at least that long."

She agreed, and didn't complain while she was eating her beans.

Chapter Thirty-Four

Clint took the 2nd watch that night so that when Sally woke, he could surprise her with bacon and biscuits. Unfortunately, he wasn't that adept at making biscuits in a pan, and they came out burned—the smell of which woke her before he could.

"Where's the fire?" she asked, sitting up.

"Sorry," he said. "I was trying to surprise you."

She got up and walked to the fire, looked at the biscuits in the pan.

"What a nice thought," she said.

"Yeah, well," he said, "the only thing saving them is going to be the bacon grease."

He handed Sally a plate with bacon and the least charred biscuits he could find.

"These are delicious," she said.

"At least you can wash it down with the coffee," he said.

"No, I'm serious."

He took a bite from his own plate and was surprised to find she was right.

"Well," he said, "I guess I'm better at this than I thought."

"What will you do for your next trick?" she asked.

"I might go hunting and cook some meat tonight," he offered.

"Now that would be a good trick," she said, approvingly.

***

They rode on, unaware that Charlie One-Feather was tracking their progress. At the same time, he was leaving a trail that was easy for Nate Banks and his men to follow.

"What the hell?" Cass Pride said, looking down at the recently dug up grave. "That's the 3rd one. They're diggin' 'em up and then buryin' them again. Why?"

"Why else?" Banks asked. "They're looking for something."

"And how do we know they ain't found it yet?" Cass asked.

"Because they're still going," Banks said. "When they find what they want, they'll either turn back, or veer off and head for the closest town."

"Any idea what they're lookin' fer?" Sam Wyatt, one of the other men, asked.

"Not a clue," Banks said, truthfully. "But whatever it is, when they find it, we're going to take it away from them."

"And then what?" Cass asked.

"We head back," Banks said.

"Is that the deal?" Cass asked.

"That's the deal," Banks said.

"Why don't we just keep goin'?" Wyatt asked. "I mean, if it's somethin' valuable."

Banks looked back at him.

"Because that isn't the deal," he said, coldly.

"And Nate Banks is a man of his word," Cass said, "aint'cha, Nate?"

"That's right."

Cass wondered just how valuable a something they were talking about, and how much it would take to make Nathaniel Banks break his word?

***

On the 4th day Clint reined in as they topped a rise.

"What is it?" Sally asked.

"I'm thinking when we come down off this rise we'll be at the point where the trail splits," he explained to her. "Would there have been any reason your father would have chosen to follow the Mormon Trail?"

"No," Sally said, "I never heard anything about that."

"What about the California Trail?"

"I think if she was going to leave the wagon train at any point it probably would've been to go to California, but as far as I know, we never got there. Besides, my father died before she could be faced with that decision."

"Then we might've passed it already," he said. "Your father's grave site."

Sally's exasperation became plain on her pretty face.

"I don't know what to do," she said.

"I do," he said. "We'll camp here and make the decision in the morning."

"But there's still daylight isn't there?"

"Yes," he said, "but we don't want to go any further until we make a decision."

"All right," she said.

"Also," he added, "they may have something to do with our decision."

"Who?" She looked at him.

"Them." He pointed.

There was another rise across from them, and at the top of that one stood 6 riders, maybe more.

"Are those . . . Indians?"

"Yup."

The only Indians Sally had ever seen—or could re-member seeing—were civilized Indians in Denver, the ones that stood out in front of stores trying to entice people to come inside. If the wagon train she and her mother were on had encountered any, she was too young to remember.

"W-what kind are they?"

"Too far to tell," he said, "but the way things are right now, it could be any combination of young braves who don't want to stay on their reservations."

"So what do we do?"

"We might be able to trade with them."

"You can do that?"

Clint looked at her, saw the concern on her face.

"Let's hope so."

Chapter Thirty-Five

They camped, picketed the horses and built a fire. There was nothing to hide, not with the Indians on the next rise—if they were still there.

They had bacon and beans again, but Sally didn't complain this time. She was too worried about the Indians.

"Would they sneak into camp at night to try and rob us? Or kill us?"

"No."

"Because Indians don't fight at night?" she asked. "Something about not being able to find their way to the happy hunting ground?"

"That's an old wives' tale."

"Damn," she said. "I was hoping that was true. It's the only thing I thought I knew about Indians."

"Don't worry," Clint said, "they'll try to bargain before they try to take."

"I hope you're right."

"If they do show up tonight, we'll just offer to let them eat with us."

"That's something I didn't expect to do this trip," she admitted. "Eat with Indians. Have you done it?"

"Many times."

"Oh?"

"I've known a lot of Indians."

"Friendly ones?"

"And the other kind."

"What tribes do you think they're from?" Sally asked.

"Who knows?" he asked. "Pawnee, Sioux, Kiowa. We'll find out, eventually."

"You seem very calm."

"The Indian wars have been over for a long time," he said. "They may not even approach us."

She looked down at her plate of bacon and beans.

"You mean I don't have to save some of this for them?"

***

Charlie One-Feather made a cold camp. He could smell the coffee and bacon from the camp ahead of him. Behind him he knew that Nate Banks and the others would be camping for the night. They'd be sitting around a warm fire.

Charlie had read the sign of the Indian ponies ahead of him. Clint Adams and his lady friend's tracks mixed in with them. He wondered if the Gunsmith was that good a tracker. Maybe not, since he wasn't tracking, he was looking for graves.

Charlie was going to lay back the next day, see what happened when the Gunsmith crossed tracks with the Indian ponies. This job might end up being over before Adams and the woman got to what they were looking for.

***

"Are you sure we're goin' the right way?" Cass asked Nate Banks.

"Charlie's leaving a trail a blind man could follow, Cass," Banks told him.

"That so? How come I can't see it, and you can?"

"Because I'm not blind," Banks said.

"You sayin' I am?"

"Why are we having this conversation?" Banks asked.

The others laughed, beans spewing from one of their mouths.

"Take it easy," Cass told them. "You might choke to death."

"Take it easy, Cass," Banks said. "Just eat your supper. Believe me, we're on the right track."

"When are we gonna get what we want?" Cass asked. "I'm gettin' impatient."

"We'll get what we want when they find what they want," Banks said.

"And what if they don't find it?"

"Then none of us is going to make any money," Banks told him.

"So this could all be for nothin'?" Cass asked.

"Possibly."

Cass looked at the other men.

"And that's okay with you fellas?"

Manfred Lee looked at Cass and said, "what the hell else we got to do?" and kept eating.

"See?" Banks said. "Now just eat."

***

Clint took the first watch, let Sally get to sleep—or, at least try to. She was restless and he knew it was because she was nervous.

"Try and relax," he called to her. "Get some sleep. You're going to need it."

"I'm afraid if I go to sleep, I might not wake up," she said, propping herself up on an elbow. "Is it true Indians scalp white people?"

"It might be true," he said, "but they didn't start it."

"What? Who did?"

"The whites."

"What?"

"Used to be a price on their heads, so white men started taking scalps to prove their kill. They didn't want to have to start lugging bodies back in as proof."

"Oh my God," she said. "Our people were that savage?"

"Some of them were, yeah," he said.

"Jesus," she said, lying back. "Now when I get home, I still won't be able to go to sleep."

But moments after that, her breathing evened out and he knew she was asleep.

He poured himself a cup of coffee and scraped the last of the bacon and beans into a plate. He really didn't mind eating them every day on the trail.

Chapter Thirty-Six

"Clint!"

He heard Sally the first time, but didn't turn over right away. He had let her sleep an extra hour or thereabouts, so now he was trying to steal an extra wink or two.

"Uh, Clint," she called, again. "We've got company."

This time he rolled over, saw the 6 Indians sitting on their horses, staring at them. Why did it seem like there was always groups of 6 coming after him lately?

They must have ridden unshod ponies into camp nice and calmly, but scared Sally, nevertheless. He was glad she hadn't started shooting.

He got to his feet, walked over to her and took the rifle.

"Leave your gun in your belt," he said, "and don't put your hand near it."

"They have rifles, too," she whispered, "I thought they used bows and arrows."

"It's a whole new world," he said. "Just relax."

"Easy for you to say."

The Indians were staring, and she could feel their eyes all over her.

He saw 2 Kiowa, 2 Pawnee, a Sioux, and 1 he couldn't recognize.

"What your name?" the Sioux asked. He sat tall on his horse, was rangy, with wide-shoulders and long legs. Clint knew if he stepped down, he'd tower over both Sally and him.

Clint was glad the brave was speaking English. He knew some Comanche from having dealt with Quanah Parker, but he was useless when it came to speaking Sioux, or Kiowa. And his experience with Pawnee was even less.

"I am Clint Adams," he said. "This is my squaw."

"What're you—" Sally started, but he shushed her.

"She tall woman."

"Yes, she is."

"She not ride well."

"No, she doesn't," Clint said. "Not yet. Would you like to step down and have some coffee? Maybe some food?"

"You have whiskey?" the brave asked.

"Sorry, no," Clint said. "We have coffee, beans, bacon—"

"Bacon?" the brave asked. He looked at the others and they nodded. "We eat bacon."

"Well, step down then," Clint said, "and I'll cook up a batch."

"You cook?" the Sioux brave asked. "Not your woman?"

"She doesn't ride well, or cook well," Clint said. He didn't want them to think Sally was good at anything. That way they wouldn't have the urge to take her away from him.

They all stepped down from their ponies, and Clint tossed a mess of bacon into a pan. He also started a fresh pot of coffee.

"We don't have enough cups for them," Sally said.

"They'll share."

"Why are you making them think I'm so helpless?" she demanded in a whisper.

He told her.

"Oh! Okay."

"Just serve the food and coffee when it's ready," Clint said.

"Should I spill it on them?"

"No!" he said. "They might think it was deliberate. Just do what I tell you to do, nothing more, and we'll get out of this."

The braves didn't bother introducing themselves. They sat, cross-legged, near the fire and waited patiently for Clint to cook the bacon. He didn't have any idea if any of them had recognized his name. It might have been better if they hadn't, because then no one would want to challenge him. On the other hand, if they knew who he was, they might *not* want to challenge him. Either way might have worked for them.

When the bacon was ready, he put it into two pans and the Indian braves attacked it with their hands, stuffing their mouths. He poured two cups of coffee, and they passed the cups back and forth, burning their mouths but not caring. It wasn't often Indians got bacon and coffee.

Clint and Sally stood back and watched the red men eat.

***

Charlie One-Feather got an early start, so he was able to watch as the Indian braves rode into Clint Adams' camp. Adams was smart, cooking for them, giving them coffee. Charlie was glad, though, that he wasn't in that camp when the food and coffee ran out.

Bacon.

He could smell it.

Wished he had some himself.

He wondered if Adams would end up killing the braves, or if they could end up killing Adams, and taking the woman.

As the braves ate, Clint was wondering the same thing. The braves had set their rifles down beside them while they ate. It might have been smart to shoot them while they ate, but the way things stood at the moment, that would be murder. They had not made a threatening move or gesture.

By the time they finished eating they had bacon grease all over their faces.

The Sioux looked up at Clint and asked, "More?"

"I'm sorry," Clint said. "You ate all that we had. How about some more coffee?"

The Sioux and others looked at each other, then they all grabbed their rifles and stood up.

"What else you got?" the Sioux asked.

"I could give you some coffee—"

"Not know how to make coffee," the Sioux said. "We want your squaw. She will make coffee."

"What?" Sally said, moving to stand behind Clint.

This was what he had been afraid would happen, and now he had to deal with it.

Chapter Thirty-Seven

"I can't do that," Clint said. "I need my squaw."

"Why need?" the Sioux asked. "Don't cook, don't ride, don't do anything."

"Then why do you want her?" Clint asked.

"She make coffee."

"I made the coffee," Clint said.

The Sioux smiled, and said, "Then she make us happy," and the other braves all laughed.

"Clint—" Sally said.

"Look," Clint said, "we've got some beans, some peaches—"

"What peaches?" the Sioux asked.

"It's fruit in a can."

"What can?"

"Sally, get a few cans."

She rushed to the gunny sacks and came back with 3 cans of peaches.

"Peaches," Clint said, handing the Sioux 1 can.

He took it, stared at it, shook it and listened, then asked, "How eat?"

"Watch." Clint took out a knife, took the can back from the Sioux, sawed it open, then speared one of the peaches out of the nectar.

He handed the Sioux the knife and said, "There, taste."

The Sioux took a bite, chewed, handed the knife to one of the Kiowa braves, who also bit into it. He handed it to the other Kiowa, while wiping nectar from his chin.

"You can eat them, and then drink the juice," Clint said, handing the can to the Sioux. "But be careful of the lid, it's sharp."

The Sioux lifted the can to his lips, sipped, then sipped again and nodded. He turned and exchanged some words with the others, then looked at Clint.

"We take peaches," he said, "you keep squaw."

"That's fine," Clint said. "I'll even throw in a bag of coffee and show you how to make it."

Clint collected all the peaches they had—he hadn't even had a chance to give Sally any—and then took the Sioux and one of the Kiowa braves and showed them how to prepare the coffee. Since he had bought an extra coffee pot, he was able to give them one, along with one of the gunny sacks.

While he was doing that, he saw the other braves looking around the camp, obviously for something else they could ask for. He had 2 fears. First, that one of them might still want Sally, and second, that one of them might want Eclipse. A couple—the Pawnee and the one he couldn't identify—kept looking over at the horses.

Finally, the coffee lesson was over and they had their booty in the gunny sack.

The braves walked to their horses, but did not mount. They talked amongst themselves, seemed to argue, and then the Sioux turned back to Clint.

Here it comes, he thought.

***

Charlie One-Feather watched the action in Clint Adams' camp, and if the Gunsmith didn't know what was coming, he did. He decided to get a little closer.

***

"I am Sharp Arrow," the Sioux said, introducing himself for the first time. "My Kiowa brothers want more than peaches and coffee."

"The woman?" Clint asked.

Sharp Arrow shook his head.

"The horse."

"Which one?" Clint might have been willing to give them Sally's horse, then ride double with her until they could get her another one. But he knew that wasn't going to be the case.

"The big one."

"That's my horse," Clint said. "They can't have him."

The Sioux returned to his Kiowa brothers and argued some more, then came back.

"They are not happy."

"Neither am I," Clint said. "I've given you all I'm going to give you, Sharp Arrow. Tell them that. It's time for us to move on. You go your way, and we'll go ours."

"I, too, wish to go my way," Sharp Arrow said. "I will tell them."

He went back to talk to the others. Clint turned to face Sally.

"What's going to happen?" she asked.

"Well, they're not going to get you and they're not going to get Eclipse."

"What about my horse? Would they take that one?"

"The Kiowa know horses," Clint said. "That's why they want mine."

"So what will they do?"

"That's what we're going to find out."

He turned as Sharp Arrow returned.

"We go!" the Sioux said.

He turned and went to the horses, where the other braves had already mounted and were waiting. The Pawnee was holding the sack with their goods. Sharp Arrow mounted up, and they all turned their horses and rode away.

"Oh my God!" she said. "I'm so glad they're gone."

"I don't know . . ." Clint said, still looking after the braves as they rode off.

"What do you mean?"

"I mean I think we should saddle up and get out of here," Clint said, "before they change their minds and come back."

"You think that might happen?" Sally asked.

"I think I don't want to wait around to find out," Clint said.

Chapter Thirty-Eight

Charlie One-Feather was close enough to have heard what was said at the end. He was sure the 2 Kiowa were not ready to give up, just yet. Not when there was a horse like the Gunsmith's Darley Arabian in their sights.

As the braves rode away, One-Feather walked to his own horse and mounted up. He would withdraw now, to a safe distance, and wait for Clint Adams' next move.

**

Clint and Sally hurriedly broke camp, saddled up and got moving again. Sally kept swiveling her neck around, making Clint think she was going to sprain it.

"Take it easy, Sally," he said.

"You said they might come back."

"If they do, they'll be in front of us," Clint said. "So just keep looking ahead."

They topped the next rise, where they had first seen the six braves, then went down the other side.

"We're going to have to stop for supplies," he told her. "Now that we gave up some of ours to those braves."

"Peaches?" she asked. "How did you know they'd like them?"

"They're sweet, and not in any Indian's daily meal," he said. "I was just hoping it would work."

"Maybe it did," she said, "on four of them."

"We'll see," Clint said. "If they're going to come at us again, it'll be soon."

***

They rode a couple more hours, Clint wondering if they should change direction, retrace their steps, or stop at a town first.

They followed the Platte River for hours, riding along the muddy south side of it, until they reached Ash Hollow. From there it would be a deep descent down Windless Hill.

"Why aren't there any tracks from the wheels?"

"There hasn't been a wagon train through here in over thirty years," Clint pointed out.

"Yes, but there were so many, I'd think there were permanent ruts left by all those wagons."

"We'll find some, in places," Clint assured her, "but eventually, most fade."

"Where are we?" she asked.

"Ash Hollow," he said. "As soon as we go down the hill, I think there's a town—what's wrong?"

She had tears in her eyes suddenly.

"My mother mentioned Ash Hollow," she said.

"Are you sure?"

"I'm positive."

"Did she say he died when the wagon train reached here?" Clint asked.

"She said it was flat and hard where he died," she went on, as if memories were suddenly flooding in. "She said they had to wait until they reached . . . yes, it was Ash Hollow . . . before they could bury him."

"Then we're here," Clint said. "His grave has to be around here, somewhere."

"Oh my God," she said, "we found him?"

"Not yet," he said, "but if your memory's correct . . . let's look around."

They turned their horses to retrace their steps just a bit, but stopped when they saw the Indians.

"Clint?"

"Take it easy," Clint said, watching the braves. "There are only two this time, the two Kiowa. They want Eclipse."

"Or me," she said.

"Or both."

"But where are the others?" She looked around.

"Maybe the others actually were satisfied with the peaches and coffee," Clint suggested.

"What are they doing?" she asked. "They're just sitting there."

"Let's not wait to find out," Clint said.

***

Charlie One-Feather was also watching, convinced that he had been right. But if the Gunsmith was killed, then whatever it was Nate Banks was looking for would go unfound.

He drew his rifle from its scabbard and waited.

***

It was Clint's turn to look around. He couldn't quite accept that these 2 Kiowa had gone off on their own. The other 4 had to be around, somewhere. He would like to have ridden up to the Kiowa, but he wasn't comfortable leaving Sally behind. And if the odds were still 6-to-1, he might have to press her into service with the Colt New Line.

"Remember how you fired at those tree trunks when we practiced?" he asked.

"Y-yes."

"If it comes to that. Just think of these Indians as tree trunks with legs. Fire at the thickest part of them."

"A-all right."

"Come on."

He started Eclipse forward at a walk, and she followed. The 2 Kiowa stood their ground, didn't move.

"Where are the other four?" Sally asked.

"That's what I'm wondering," Clint admitted.

"Shouldn't we take our guns out?" she asked. "Show them to them?"

"They know we have guns," Clint said. "They don't seem to particularly care. All you have to do is start firing when I do. Understand?"

"I understand," she said, "but I don't know how much good I'll do you."

"Just make noise," Clint said, "and when your gun is empty, hit the ground and lie flat."

"I can do that."

Suddenly, Clint saw 2 more braves, the Pawnee, just on the other side of the river, to their left.

"Clint . . ."

"I see them."

Then, to the right, Sharp Arrow appeared, riding with the brave Clint couldn't identify.

"To our right," he said.

She looked and caught her breath.

"I guess they weren't satisfied with the coffee and peaches," he said.

"What do we do?" she asked, urgently.

"I'm going to have to take out the two Kiowa in front of us pretty quickly," he said. "That way I can cut the odds down to 4-to-1."

"Don't you mean 4-to-2?" she asked.

He turned his head and looked at her, she had her chin up and her shoulders squared.

"Yes, Sally," he said, "that's exactly what I mean. Let's cut the odds down to 4-to-2."

Chapter Thirty-Nine

They had one advantage. 2 of the Indian braves were on the other river bank. They would have to ride across to be effective.

Clint and Sally continued to ride toward the 2 Kiowa, their horses' hooves making wet, sucking noises in the muddy ground.

"When do we do something?" she asked.

"Take it easy," Clint said. "Let's see what they do."

To their right, the braves kept pace with them. Across the river, the others did the same. There was no imminent danger at that moment. Clint decided if they got close enough to the Kiowa before anyone made a move, they would talk.

When they got within earshot Clint reined in. The other braves did the same. Now they all simply sat astride their horses, nobody making a move.

"What do you want?" Clint asked.

The 2 Kiowa looked at each other, then 1 of them pointed at Clint's horse.

"I already told you, you can't have him," Clint said.

The other Kiowa pointed at Sally.

"You can't have her, either."

Clint could hear Sally breathing—and then she stopped, holding her breath. When the Kiowa started to bring their rifles up, Clint drew and fired.

At that moment the braves on either side of them also started to fire. Sally drew her gun, almost dropped it, closed her eyes and started pulling the trigger.

Clint's shots took both Kiowa right off their horses, forcing them over backwards. They fell into the mud and didn't move.

He turned to his right, saw Sharp Arrow and the other brave coming toward them, firing their rifles. Sally stopped firing.

"Hit the ground!" he shouted. "Lay flat."

"But . . . the mud!"

A bullet whizzed past her ear and she immediately leaped from the saddle into the gooey mud and lay flat.

Clint heard shots from the other side of the river, but knew he had to deal with the 2 on his side first.

He had 4 shots left, was going to have to make them count before pressing his rifle into service.

Raising his gun, he waited until they got closer, lead flying past him, before pulling the trigger twice.

The brave he could never identify was jerked from his horse as if from behind. As he hit the ground Clint fired at the Sioux, but at that moment the man's pony stumbled, went to his knees, then regained his stride. The move had caused Clint's bullet to miss.

Sharp Arrow was still coming, so Clint holstered his pistol and pulled his rifle free. Concerned that the other 2 were now riding across the river and getting closer, he raised his rifle and fired. The bullet Struck Sharp Arrow in the chest, and he fell from his horse.

At that moment Clint felt a chunk of hot lead hit him from behind, in the left shoulder. He turned Eclipse and saw that the 2 Pawnee were closer than he'd thought. Suddenly, there was rifle fire from another direction, and both men were dumped into the river.

There were no more shots.

"Can I get up?" Sally called.

Clint looked down at her, lying in the mud, staring up at him. The whites of her eyes stood out from the brown goo that covered her face.

"Yes," he said, "get up."

He turned Eclipse to see where the shots had come from. Another Indian, a man wearing trail clothes rather than the loin cloths the other braves had been wearing, was coming toward them. He was also wearing a black hat with one single feather on it.

Clint kept his rifle in his hand, as he hadn't had the time to reload his Peacemaker.

The Indian approached them and reined in.

"Are you all right?" the man asked.

"I think so," Clint said.

"You're bleeding!" Sally said, standing up.

Abruptly, Clint felt the burning sensation in his left shoulder, but the wound didn't feel life threatening.

"I think I'll be all right," he said.

"I can have a look," the Indian said. He spoke perfect English.

"Who are you?" Clint asked.

"Sorry," the man said. "My name's Charlie. I heard the shots, saw that you were outnumbered, so I thought I'd lend a hand."

"I'm glad you did," Clint said. "Thanks."

They all looked around, didn't see any of the 6 Indians stirring.

"I suppose you better have a look at my shoulder, then," Clint said. He looked at Sally. "And you better wash off in the river."

Chapter Forty

Charlie pronounced Clint's shoulder wound a minor one, and patched him up the best he could, using an extra shirt that Clint had in his saddlebags.

"Now we need coffee," he told Sally, "and a shirt."

Sally, still drying off from cleaning up in the river, shivered and said, "I'm just glad you're all right."

"So where were you two headed before those men tried to waylay you?"

"Uh, nowhere, really—" Sally started, but Clint cut her off.

"I think there's a town called Schylerville near here," Clint said. "That's where we're headed."

"Well," Charlie said, "I'm goin' the other way, so unless you want help burying these men—"

"That's okay," Clint said. "I think we'll just let them lie where they are."

"I don't blame you for that," Charlie said. "Be seein' you."

"Thanks again," Clint said, as Charlie walked to his horse and mounted up.

"By the way," Clint called, before Charlie could ride off.

"Yeah?"

"There was one brave I couldn't identify," he said. "Do you know what tribe he was from?"

Since Charlie had inspected each body to make sure they were dead, he did.

"He was Ponca"

"Ponca? Don't think I've ever heard of them."

"They're real local," Charlie said.

"You mind me asking how you know that?" Clint asked.

"Easy," Charlie said, with a grin. "I'm Ponca."

And he rode off.

***

Once Charlie was gone, Sally stripped off her wet clothes and dressed in the dry ones she still had in her saddlebags.

"I'm glad I didn't listen to you and snuck another pair of trousers in here," she said. "And a shirt."

"At least you have another shirt," he said. "Mine is now a bandage."

"We're going to get a doctor look at you when we get to a town."

"Well," he said, standing up, "right now we have a grave to find."

Sally was staring after Charlie, who had ridden out of sight by then.

"How do you think he just happened to come along in time?" she asked.

"Lucky, I guess," Clint said.

"Isn't Schylerville the town we passed a little ways back?" she asked. "You mentioned it when we went by."

"That's right," he said, "we passed it, but it's still the nearest town."

"But didn't he say he was going in the opposite direction?" she asked.

Now he stared in the direction Charlie had ridden, and realized what she was getting at.

"You're right."

"Then why's he headed for Schylerville?"

"Good question," Clint said.

***

They got themselves mounted and spent an hour riding around the area, looking for possible grave sites.

"Okay," Clint said, at that point, "I guess we better head in the direction of Schylerville.

"Maybe we'll run into our new friend," she said. "Why do you think he helped us, and then lied to us?"

"I don't know," Clint said. "But maybe we'll get a chance to ask him."

They rode for another hour, in concentric circles since Sally felt they were in the right place. About to give up, Clint suddenly noticed something.

"What's that?" he said.

"Where?"

He pointed. There was a flash of light, as if the sun was reflecting off something.

"Come on," Clint said. "Let's take a look."

They rode toward the flickering light with Clint trying to keep it in sight. Finally, Clint pinned it down and headed straight for it.

"What is that?" he asked.

It was something sticking up out of the ground, shaped like a headstone.

"Oh, my God!" Sally said, as they got closer. "I know what it is!"

"What?"

"It's a mirror," she said. "The kind that's attached to the back of a dresser, or a dressing table. It's from a piece of bedroom furniture."

As they got closer, Clint could see what she meant. The half circle mirror was framed in wood that had been battered by the elements for all these years. There was hardly any reflective surface that wasn't cloudy. But there was just enough to have caught the sunlight in just the right way.

They both dismounted and walked to it.

"Is this a grave?" she asked.

"It sure looks like it's meant to be a headstone," he said, putting his hand on it, "And from the condition of the mirror, it's been here a lot of years."

"So?" Sally asked. "What are we saying?"

"We're saying," Clint replied, "get the shovels!"

Chapter Forty-One

Nate Banks looked up from his coffee cup when he heard a rider coming.

"It's Charlie," Cass announced. "It's about time!"

Banks stood up and waited for Charlie to reach the camp. The others crowded behind him.

Charlie One-Feather was off his horse even before it came to a stop. Quietly, he explained the situation to Banks.

"You did what?" Cass asked.

"I saved his life," Charlie said. "Him and the woman. Those six braves would've killed them if I hadn't taken a hand."

"You did the right thing, Charlie," Banks said. "What happened after that?"

"After I bandaged him up, I left, but I kept watchin'," he said. "They ain't leavin' that area. They're ridin' around, searchin'. I think that's where they're gonna find . . . whatever it is you want them to find."

"That's it, then," Banks said. "Saddle up. When they find it, I want us to be there."

"Find what?" Cass asked. He looked at Charlie. "You get back there fast. We'll be right behind you."

Without a word Charlie mounted up and rode back out at a breakneck speed.

***

Banks looked at Cass, the other men, then looked over at Charlie One-Feather.

"That's what we're going to find out.

***

Clint collected the 2 shovels they had, but the ground was soft, so he allowed Sally to just stand aside and watch him dig. When she objected, he told her he needed her to stand watch.

"There's no telling who else might come along," he said.

"All right, then."

The first thing he did was remove the mirror from the ground and lay it aside, then started digging. About 6 feet down he struck something that turned out to be a blanket.

"Okay, let's unwrap this," he said to her. "It's not going to be pretty."

"I'm prepared."

As he unfolded the blanket it started to fall apart in his hands. Then a skull came into view, followed by a collection of bones, but only odds and ends as a lot of the body had disintegrated over the years.

Eventually, he got what was left of the blanket, laid it on the ground, and then pulled out what remained of the bones, and skull.

"I don't know how you're going to tell," he said.

"What about the Bible?" she asked. "The leather cover?"

He got back into the hole and started rooting around with his bare hands.

"Okay, wait," he said, and pulled something out. "This looks like it might've been a leather binding."

He reached up and handed it to Sally, who cradled it against her body for a moment, then inspected at it.

"It has a cross on it," she said. "It was a Bible cover."

Clint was still digging around in the hole and came up with something else.

"Sally, did your mother tell you how your father died?" he asked.

"No, she never did."

"Did you ask her?"

"I did, but she insisted it didn't matter," she said. "He died and left us alone, and that was all she'd say. Why? What did you find?"

He held the object up in 2 fingers so she could see it.

"What is that?" she asked.

"It's a bullet," he said.

"What?"

He climbed out of the hole and stood next to her.

"Bones, a Bible, and a bullet," he said. "If this was your father's grave, then somebody shot him."

"What?"

"Looks like this bullet hit some bone, because it's misshapen. I can't tell right now if it was fired from a pistol or a rifle."

"Somebody killed my father?"

"Looks like it."

"But . . . why?"

"I don't think we'll ever find the answer to that," Clint said.

He put the bullet into his pocket.

"I'll get another blanket to wrap these remains in. Then we'll put them in one of the gunny sacks."

They had reclaimed the gunny sack they had given to the 6 Indian braves.

"Is there anything else in that hole?" she asked.

"Like what?"

"I don't know," she said, "I'm just . . . I didn't expect to find a bullet. Maybe there's . . . something else unexplainable in there."

"Well," he said, "I can take another look."

He got back in the hole and went to work with the shovel. After another foot the shovel struck something.

"What's that?" Sally asked.

Clint dug around it with the shovel, then reached down, grabbed it and pulled it free.

"It's a metal box," he said, getting out of the hole.

"Why would that be buried with my father?"

"I don't know."

"What's in it?" she asked. "Is it locked?"

"After all these years," he said, "whatever's in it has probably turned to dust."

"Can we see?"

He crouched down and placed the box on the ground. Sally crouched next to him. The box was about a foot by a foot, about 6 inches deep. He opened it, expecting nothing, but there was a tube there.

"What's that?" Sally asked.

"Looks like the kind of tube they keep spy glasses in," he said.

"Spy glass?"

"You know, a hand-held telescope that extends?"

"Oh. Is that what it is?"

He picked it up.

"No," he said, "it's not heavy enough. Looks like something else might've been put in here for safekeeping."

"Like what?"

"Let's find out."

It opened at one end. He turned it over so that whatever was inside it would slide out into his hand.

"It's a map."

"A map? Of what?"

He unrolled it carefully, not wanting it to fall apart in his hands. It seemed to be in good condition. He got it completely unfolded and held it at the top and the bottom.

"What is that?"

"It looks like a map to a gold mine," he said. "And it looks like it's located on Pike's Peak."

"Pike's Peak?"

"There was a gold rush there in the late fifties, thousands of fifty-niners rushed in to get rich."

"And did they?"

"Some did, some didn't."

"So what do you think this means?"

"It might be a map to a played-out mine," he said, "or it might be a location that hadn't been mined yet."

"Oh my God," she said. "My dad had a gold mine?"

He rolled the map up again, slid it into the tube and capped it. He didn't put it back into the metal box.

"That's what we're going to find out."

Chapter Forty-Two

Clint wasn't sure about Sally.

All along he'd had the feeling that there was something he wasn't being told. But what was it? Did Sally and Cal Morehead know about this map? And why would such a thing be buried with her father for all these years?

Clint tied the shovel back onto his saddle, while Sally took the gunny sack with her father's remnants and tied it to her saddle.

"Now what?" she asked.

"I think we're going to skip Schylerville," Clint said.

"Why?" she asked.

"Because it's the logical choice for us to go to," he said. "So instead, I think we'll keep moving forward and head for Columbus."

"What's there?"

"It's a larger town," Clint said, "and I think it'll have a telegraph office. We need to let Cal know that we found your father's grave."

"And do you want to tell him about the map?"

"Not in a telegram," Clint said. "I don't want the word to get around. We'll have to head back to Denver and tell him then."

As they mounted up, she said, "You don't think we should go to Pike's Peak?"

"We may have a map to this mine, but that doesn't mean it'll be easy to find, and it doesn't mean it won't already be played out. It'll be up to Cal to put together a team to go there and find out."

"And would you be on that team?" she asked.

"No."

"Why not?"

"My job was to get you here and get you home, and that's what I'm going to do."

"But this is gold," she said.

"I told you this wasn't about money for me," he reminded her.

"Yes, but . . . this is gold."

"I'll leave that to you and Cal," he said.

As they started to ride west again, he wondered if maybe she didn't want to share this with Cal Morehead, even though he was the payroll that got her here.

***

Charlie One-Feather got back before Clint and Sally packed up to leave. Now he watched as they left the grave uncovered. He assumed there were no remains left there.

They must have been in the bag the woman tied to her saddle.

He looked behind him, waiting for Nate Banks and the others to appear. But when Clint Adams and the woman stated riding west, he had to stay with them. Apparently, they weren't going to Schylerville. If they were headed for Columbus, it would give Nate and the others more time to catch up.

***

Clint and Sally rode in silence for some time, each alone with their thoughts. It was Sally who broke the silence.

"Clint?"

"Yes?"

"What if I don't want to go back to Denver?"

He looked at her.

"Why not?"

"Well," she said, "I think I've been happier all this time with you than I ever have been there."

"Sally, I don't think—"

"Don't get scared," she said, cutting him off. "I'm not saying I'm in love with you. It's just . . . that life is not the one I want."

"And what about Cal Morehead?"

"I don't want him, either."

"But he wants you," Clint said. "and he bankrolled this whole trip."

"I know," she said. "I suppose I'll have to try to make him understand."

"And what about the map? And the mine?"

She hesitated, then asked, "Do we have to tell him about them?"

"Sally—"

She cut him off, again.

"No, I mean, we did all the work," she pointed out. "You and I could go and see this mine, and if it's worth it, we can work it. You keep saying money means nothing to you, so I bet you'd have the money to hire some men to work it for us."

"That's not the point, Sally," Clint said. "I've got to go back to Denver and finish what I started with Cal Morehead. Once that's done, if you and he want to go your separate ways, that's your business."

"Are you going to tell him about the map?"

"I'm going to tell him that we found the grave," Clint said, "and that you have your father's remains. And by the way, wasn't this all so you could take him back there and bury him beside your mother?"

"Well, yes . . ."

"So then we have to go back," Clint said. "I'll leave it up to you whether or not you want to tell him about the map. As far as I'm concerned, it was buried with your father, so it belongs to you."

She thought a moment, then nodded and said, "Okay, I can live with that."

"I'm glad we got that settled," he said.

"So am I," she said.

They rode for a few minutes before Clint asked, "So your mother never said a thing about a map?"

"Not to me."

"And there's nothing in the letters I read," he said. "I wonder if the map could've been tossed into the grave by someone else."

"Why?" she asked.

"Maybe they intended to come back and get it."

"And never did?"

"Maybe they couldn't," he said. "Your father died on the wagon train. Other people did, too, I'm sure. Could be one of them threw the map into the grave when nobody was looking."

"If that's true, then nobody else is looking for it," she said. "It really is ours."

"Yours."

"But we found it together."

"It's all yours, Sally, believe me."

"What do you have against gold?" she asked.

"I've seen it ruin many men," he said.

"Friends?"

"Some," Clint said, "others were partners."

"So you've been involved in mining?"

"A time or two," he said. "They didn't turn out well."

"I'd be a good partner for you," Sally said. "Don't you think?"

"All my partners started out good," he said. "Then they saw the gold."

"I'm sure we could come to an understanding," she said.

"I don't think so."

"I'm just asking you to give it some thought."

"Sure."

"I never met a man who seemed so dead set against getting rich," she said.

"I don't like rich people very much," he said. "they're different."

"And if you got rich, you'd change?"

He looked straight ahead.

"I don't want to find out."

Chapter Forty-Three

Nate Banks and the others finally caught up to Charlie One-Feather.

"Where are they?" Banks asked.

"Just ahead," Charlie said.

"Where are they goin'?"

"I think to Columbus," Charlie said. "It's the first town they'll come to."

"Not headin' for Schylerville?"

"No."

"What's in Columbus?"

"A bank," Charlie said, "some saloons, restaurants . . . and a telegraph office."

"Telegraph office," Nate Banks repeated. "If they're working for somebody, they'll want to contact him."

"That makes sense," Cass said.

"So we're going to stop them before they get there," Banks went on.

"That makes sense, too," Charlie said.

"Charlie," Banks said, "can you get ahead of them without them seeing you?"

"No problem," Charlie One-Feather said.

"Then here's what I want you to do."

***

When Clint reined in, Sally looked up from her reverie in surprise. She had been trying to make up her mind about something, and Clint had left her alone with her thoughts.

"Why are we stopping?" she asked.

"Look." He pointed ahead of them.

She saw a rider, just sitting still on his horse.

"Is that?"

"Yes," he said, "our savior, Charlie."

"What's he doing there?" she asked. "He rode the other way?"

"Obviously, he figured out where we're going, and got ahead of us."

"But why?"

"That's what we're about to find out."

Clint started forward again, at a slow gait, and Sally fell into step.

As they approached, Charlie the Ponca Indian turned his horse sideways, this way his rifle—which was being held across the saddle—was pointing at them as they reached him. When Clint reined in again, he did the same thing.

"Hello, Charlie."

"Adams."

"Did I tell you my name when we met?" Clint asked.

"You didn't have to," Charlie said. "I knew."

"What's going on, Charlie?"

"Some friends of mine are interested in talking to you," Charlie said.

"What friends might those be?" Clint asked.

"Those," Charlie said, gesturing with his left hand, while maintaining the hold on his rifle with his right.

He was pointing behind them so Clint shifted his eyes, able to look that way without turning his head. He saw 5 men on horses approaching.

"Stop them, Charlie."

"I can't."

"You have to," Clint said. "I can't let them get closer without killing you first. Unless you stop them, and we talk."

Charlie didn't move.

"If you know who I am, Charlie, you know I can kill you, even if you kill me, too."

After half a second Charlie raised a hand, and the riders stopped.

"Now what's going on, Charlie?" Clint asked. "Why save our necks and then do this?"

Charlie shrugged. "It's what I'm being paid to do."

"Paid by who?"

"That man."

Clint looked at the group of men sitting their horses behind them.

"The one in the lead?"

Charlie nodded.

"Can you bring him over here without the others?"

Charlie nodded, raised his hand again, with 1 finger showing. The leader started forward again, stopped about 20 feet away.

"I understand you're in charge," Clint said.

"That's right."

"What's your name?"

"Nate Banks."

"What's this about?"

"It's about what you took out of that hole back there," the man said.

"And what's that?"

"Don't play games, Adams," Banks said. "I want it. Hand it over."

Clint studied the man, convinced that he had no idea what they had taken from the hole.

"Give it to him," Clint said to Sally.

"What?"

"Give him the sack, Sally," Clint said. "Toss it to him."

"No, no," Banks said. "I ain't that dumb. She'll toss it and you'll shoot me while I'm catching it. Let Charlie bring it over."

That suited Clint, since that would mean they were no longer in a crossfire between Charlie and Banks.

"Do it," he said.

Charlie rode over to Sally and took the gunny sack from her when she untied it from her saddle. He then rode to Banks and handed it to him. Now they were side-by-side. Infinitely better.

Banks untied the sack and looked inside. He frowned, then turned the sack over and dumped the contents onto the ground.

"What's the gag?" he asked. "It's a bunch of bones."

"What else did you think we'd find in a grave?"

"Jimmy didn't say anything about any bones," Banks said.

"Jimmy Nash?" Clint asked. "He sent you?"

Banks remained silent, realizing he'd misspoken.

"And it was probably him and Felix, right?" Clint asked. "The only two old enough to remember the last wagon train."

"They said the wagonmaster buried something," Banks said. "I want it."

"That's it," Clint said, indicating the bones on the ground. "That's her father. She wants to take him home and bury him next to her mother. That's it. That's why we're here."

"No, that's a lie," Banks said. "Those two old geezers are after something that's worth money."

"Okay, Banks," Clint said, "this can go one of two ways."

"How do you figure?"

"Well, you and Charlie are sitting side-by-side, now," Clint said. "You had me in a crossfire, but he moved. Now I can kill the two of you easily. I do that, those others are going to turn around and ride off."

"How does that figure?"

"They don't even know as much as you do," Clint said, "and you know next to nothing. But you probably told them who I am. I'm going to impress the hell out of them by drawing and firing, killing you two before you can move. Believe me, they'll turn around and leave."

Clint could see Banks' mind racing. Charlie, on the other hand, was just waiting to be told what to do.

"What's the other way?" Banks asked.

"You two can turn now and ride away," Clint said, "and it'll be all over. Tell those two old geezers you didn't get what they wanted."

Banks stared at Clint, his eye flicking from side-to-side as he tried to make a decision.

"Charlie?" Clint said. "I owe you, so why don't you just ride away?"

Charlie stared at Clint, but remained alongside Nate Banks.

"Charlie did what he did to keep you alive until I caught up," Banks said. Clint's speaking directly to Charlie seemed to have made Banks' mind up for him. "Charlie One-Feather is my man, not yours."

"That's too bad," Clint said. "I've never killed a man within hours of him saving my life, but I guess that's the way it's going to have to be."

Banks looked at Charlie, then at Clint. Suddenly, he turned his horse around, followed by the Ponca Indian. Clint slid his rifle back into its scabbard, because whatever happened now, he was going to use his Peacemaker. He probably should have shot the 2 men, and not let them return to the side of the others.

"Get ready with your gun, Sally."

"Oh, Lord," she breathed.

If they all started riding toward him and Sally, it would be worse than the situation with the Indians earlier. There would be no Charlie One-Feather coming to their aid.

But if his decision was wrong, Banks' was even worse. For suddenly he and Charlie whirled around, drew their guns, and started riding toward Clint.

Chapter Forty-Four

Clint didn't move.

"Clint?" Sally said.

"Wait."

He was sure the 2 men would be firing at him first. They would want Sally alive to tell them what was in that grave besides her father's bones.

The 2 men started to fire, and Clint stood his ground.

"Clint."

"Don't move," he repeated, "don't breathe, and don't draw your gun. Just sit."

She watched with wide eyes.

***

"What the hell—" one of the other men said, as Banks and Charlie started back toward them. "What should we do?"

"Just wait," Cass said.

"For what?"

"Just wait," Cass said. "That's the Gunsmith. I wanna watch."

That's when Banks and Charlie turned.

***

Clint watched, figured Charlie was his biggest threat. The Ponca Indian was lifting his rifle into position, while Banks drew his pistol. He had to make a split-second decision.

He drew and fired twice, not quickly, but accurately.

The first bullet struck Banks in the chest. Blood exploded from him as his mouth opened, he dropped his gun, and then tumbled from the saddle.

Clint hated to do it, but the second bullet struck Charlie One-Feather in the forehead, knocking his one-feathered hat off his head before he fell to the ground. Their horses continued running and rumbled past Clint and Sally.

Clint kept his gun in his hand and waited for the other 4 men to make their decision.

***

"Jesus!" one of the men breathed, as Banks and Charlie fell from their horses a split second apart.

Clint didn't feel he had drawn and fired quickly, but to the 4 men watching, it was quicker than they could follow.

"What do we do?" one of the men said aloud.

"We get the hell outta here!" Cass said.

He turned his horse and as he rode hell-bent-for-leather away, the others followed.

***

"God," Sally said.

"Are you all right?" Clint asked.

"Yes," she said. "I was so scared."

"Stay right there."

He rode up to check the 2 bodies, then dismounted, put the remains of Sally's father back into the sack, rode back and handed it to her.

"Where's the map?" she asked. "I thought it was in there, but then I realized you wouldn't tell me to give it to them if it was."

"In my saddlebags," he said.

"God," she said, again, "I'm so glad I made this trip with *you*. I don't know if we'd be alive now if it was anyone else."

"I'm sorry about Charlie," he said. "Even though it was for the wrong reason, he did save our lives."

"You had no choice," she said. "Do you think those others will come back?"

"No," Clint said, "they're done. All we have to do now is get back to Denver."

"Clint—"

"You can decide what you want to do once we get there, Sally," Clint said.

"I understand."

"Now let's get to Columbus, send Cal a telegram," he said, "and just go from there."

They turned their horses and headed west again.

Chapter Forty-Five

Denver

Clint came down to the lobby of The Denver House and found Talbot Roper waiting for him.

"You know," he said, "if you had been here weeks ago, I wouldn't have gone looking for the last wagon train."

"I know," Roper said, "it was all my fault."

"Did you get the information I needed?" Clint asked.

"If you buy me breakfast," Roper said, "I just might tell you."

"Eating here okay?"

"It's fine," Roper said. "They have a great dining-room."

"I know."

They walked across the lobby, entered the diningroom and were shown to the table Clint usually sat at—in a corner, from where he could see the entire room, away from the windows.

The waiter came over and they both ordered steak and eggs. The waiter poured coffee and then went to get their steaks.

"Okay," Clint said, "What have you got?"

"Okay," Roper said, opening the file he was holding. "Cyrus Elliot, wagonmaster for about twenty years, until he took what's generally considered to be the last wagon train out."

"I could've guessed that."

"Well, before he started taking wagon trains across country, he was a miner."

"Ah . . ."

"It gets better," Roper said. "He had a partner named Henry Webster."

"Webster?"

Roper nodded.

"He was on that last wagon train with his family, but he didn't make it."

"Died?"

Roper nodded.

"How?"

"According to Elliot, he just keeled over. They buried him along the way."

"Everybody believed him?"

"Why not?" Roper asked. "He was the wagonmaster. Why, you know different?"

Clint took a bullet from his pocket and said, "I do."

The waiter came with breakfast.

"Before we start eating," Clint said, "Webster and El-liot were partners in what?"

"Well," Roper said, "in a few instances, a gold mine."

"I thought you might say that. But they weren't part-ners at this time?"

"Nope," Roper said, "they had parted company a few years before."

"So was it a coincidence that Webster was on Elliot's last wagon train?"

"Normally, I'd say yes," Roper said, "but you hate coincidences."

"I do," Clint said. "Let's eat."

"I've got one more thing for you," Roper said.

"What's that?"

Instead of speaking, Roper simply handed the file over and allowed Clint to read for himself.

***

When Clint got to the Immigrant Saloon, the front doors were open. He entered and saw Wendell standing behind the bar. It was early, and nobody else was around. When he saw Clint, he smiled.

"Beer?" he asked. "Or is it too early."

"Well, I had a big breakfast," Clint said. "One won't hurt me."

"Never will," Wendell agreed, and set one up for him.

"Have you seen Sally this morning?" Clint asked.

"Haven't you heard?"

"Heard what?"

"She's gone."

"Gone? Where? When?"

"Well," Wendell said, "you got back two days ago, so she left yesterday."

"Just . . . left?"

"Packed up and went," Wendell said. "You didn't know?"

"I had no idea."

"Then maybe you should tell Mr. Morehead," Wendell said. "He thinks you did. In fact, he thinks you might be meeting her."

"Is he in his office?"

"Yeah," Wendell said, "he's tryin' to decide whether or not he should hire somebody to kill you."

"Trying to decide?" Clint asked. "She left yesterday, and he hasn't decided yet?"

"Well," Wendell said, "his best man is dead."

"Donaldson?"

Wendell nodded.

"I guess I better talk to him before he finds another man."

"Go on up."

Clint took his beer to the stairs with him and made his way up to Morehead's door.

"Go away!" the man yelled, when he knocked.

"It's Clint Adams."

After a moment Morehead said, "Come on in."

Clint opened the door and went in, found himself looking down the barrel of a small gun Morehead held in his hand.

"Put it down, Cal," he said, "it's not your style."

Morehead hesitated, then said, "You're right." He put the gun down. "I hire other people to do my killing." He sat back in his chair, shoulders slumped.

"Well, before you hire somebody else to kill me you better read this."

"What is it?"

Clint stepped to the desk and handed Morehead the file Roper had given him.

"The map of the gold mine we found had been in Sally's family a long time," he said. "Henry Webster had been partners with a man named Cyrus Elliot for years. Eventually, they went their separate ways. But then Webster showed up on a wagon train where Elliot was the wagonmaster. Foolishly, Webster waved the map in Elliot's face. So Elliot shot Webster, but told everybody he simply keeled over. He buried Webster, and the map. Probably figured his next time over the trail he'd dig it up. Only what he didn't know was, that was the last wagon train."

"Why didn't he go back, anyway?"

"Before he could," Clint said, "he died."

"So the map stayed buried all these years."

"Until Sally decided to go and get it."

"She knew about it?"

"I'm sure she did," Clint said. "I kept feeling there was something I wasn't being told. I thought it was you, but it was her. Her mother probably told her about it when she died."

"That was a year ago," Morehead said, "Why'd she wait so long?"

"She had to convince you to pay for it, and get some-body she thought she could count on to go with her."

"So she used us both?"

"Oh yeah, she did."

"And what about Rafe Donaldson?" Morehead asked. "Who killed him?"

"I don't think I'm going out on a limb to say she did," he said. "I don't know what happened between them, but he ended up dead in her compartment. She probably couldn't move him, so she came to me with the story about finding him."

"But why kill him at all?"

Clint shrugged.

"Maybe he was in her way. Or she didn't have him wrapped around her little finger, so felt it was better to get rid of him before he could report back to you. She even suggested that she and I head for that mine and forget about coming back here."

"And you're not meeting her later?" Morehead asked.

"No, I'm not," Clint said. "She never asked me to, and I would have said no if she did."

Morehead was looking at the file.

"And what's this?"

"The last bit of the story I wanted you to see," Clint said. "The mine that map leads to? According to my detective friend—the best in the business—it played out a long time ago."

Morehead looked up at Clint and smiled.

"She's gonna find that out when she gets there, isn't she?" he asked, with satisfaction.

"She sure is," Clint said.

Coming January 27, 2019

THE GUNSMITH
443
Beauty and the Gun

**For more information
visit:** www.SpeakingVolumes.us

Coming December 27, 2018

Lady Gunsmith
6
Roxy Doyle and the Desperate Housewife

For more information
visit: www.SpeakingVolumes.us

On Sale Now!

THE GUNSMITH *series*
Books 430 – 441

**For more information
visit:**

On Sale Now!

Lady Gunsmith *series*
Books 1 – 5

For more information
visit: www.SpeakingVolumes.us

On Sale Now!

ANGEL EYES *series*
by Award-Winning Author
Robert J. Randisi (J.R. Roberts)

For more information
visit:

On Sale Now!

TRACKER *series*
by Award-Winning Author
Robert J. Randisi (J.R. Roberts)